"I'm not _____, his voice hu_____ feeling something for you I've never felt before."

"Zack. Don't. I...Carl and I..."

"I know. Don't you think I keep telling myself that you have a boyfriend?" He turned toward Elaine, caressing her face with his hands. "But is gratitude all you feel for Carl?"

Elaine could barely breathe, let alone think. The skin on her face burned under his touch. "There's friendship," she began shakily, struggling to find the right words. "And caring..."

"But what about love?" Zack asked softly, kissing her left cheek. "And romance?" He kissed her right cheek. "And desire?" His warm lips moved gently onto hers.

Elaine closed her eyes—falling falling falling into a world that was only Zack.

SENIORS

SWEET TALK
Created by Eileen Goudge

LAUREL-LEAF
BOOKS

Published by
Dell Publishing Co., Inc.
1 Dag Hammarskjold Plaza
New York, New York 10017

Created by Cloverdale Press
133 Fifth Avenue
New York, New York 10003

Cover photo by Pat Hill

Laurel-Leaf Library ® TM 766734,
Dell Publishing Co., Inc.

Seniors[TM] is a trademark of Dell Publishing Co., Inc.,
New York, New York.

ISBN: 0-440-98411-4

RL: 6.4

Printed in the United States of America

March 1986

10 9 8 7 6 5 4 3 2 1

WFH

Special thanks to Helen Pyne and
Cinematographic Historian Sy Sussman

For the gang at E.T.H.S. and,
most especially, Susan Sussman

Chapter One

Robin's egg blue? No. Too green.

Sky blue? No. Too pale.

What color *were* Zack's eyes? Elaine frowned at the fan of playing cards in her hand, straining to remember the *exact* color of Zack Waverly's hypnotic eyes.

Her vision blurred. Zack's face floated up from the cards. Elaine concentrated on his thick-lashed, strong, steely eyes.

"Gunmetal blue!" she said triumphantly, looking up...right into Carl Schmidt's surprised face.

"Gunmetal blue?" asked Carl, his thin body precariously balanced on the kitchen chair's back legs. His sparkling hazel eyes peered at Elaine over the tops of his cards. "Is that a new form of bidding. One club. Three hearts. Gun-metal blue?"

Elaine quickly arranged the cards in her hand according to suit. "Very funny, Carl," she said, her cheeks hot with embarrassment. It was bad enough she'd been daydreaming about Zack right in front of Carl. Did she have to *talk* about him, too? "It's just so hot in this kitchen, it's hard to concentrate." On bridge, anyway, she thought.

"Hot? Ten minutes ago I had to put my arm around you because you were so cold!"

"Well, that was ten minutes ago," snapped Elaine, angry with herself for creating excuses to get Carl to put his arm around her.

"Maybe you're coming down with some-thing," he said.

Yes, thought Elaine, like a bad case of Lack of Romance. "What I'm coming down with is a hot kitchen," she said.

"No problem," said Carl, jumping up and opening a window.

A cool late-night breeze rushed in, fluttering the deck of cards on the table. Elaine closed her eyes and held her face toward the bracing air. Maybe, with her head thrown back like this, her silky hair brushing her shoulders, her lips tilted up invitingly, Carl would be overcome with a mad, passionate desire to gather her in his arms and . . .

"Your bid," said Carl. Elaine's eyes snapped

2

open in time to see Carl swing his leg cowboy style over his chair back, settling in for another rubber of two-handed bridge.

"One club." She sighed.

The game seemed endless. Bridge wasn't at all the kind of game Elaine was interested in playing. Cards weren't what she wanted to be holding. No matter how hard Elaine tried, she couldn't keep her mind from wandering...and it always wandered straight to Zack Waverly. It wasn't that he was handsome, exactly. But he had a way about him—an offbeat humor, an easy manner—that made her feel bubbly inside when she thought of him. He was, she decided, a lot like Bill Murray in *Caddyshack*, or *Ghostbusters*, or...

"That's game!" Carl shouted triumphantly. He lifted his left eyebrow at her. "I don't know, Elaine. I've never seen you misplay so many cards. I think you lost in record time. If you ask me, your 'heart' wasn't in it."

Elaine smiled weakly at his pun. Oh, Carl, she thought guiltily, you're closer to the truth than you know. *Stop thinking of Zack*, she told herself as they sorted the cards into two decks. But how could she stop thinking about Zack when he kept calling every night for a "friendly chat"? Why did her new friend, Karen Waverly, have to have such a fascinating brother?

"...worked up a serious appetite," Carl was saying as he opened the refrigerator. "Let's see

...yogurt, carrot sticks, apples, oranges. Blech!" he said disgustedly. "Doesn't anyone *eat* in this house anymore?"

Elaine sympathized. "The fridge always looks like that after Mom takes us to the dentist," she said, running her tongue over her newest filling. "The twins had a cavity apiece, and Andrea may have one starting under her braces."

"But I'm *starving*." Carl flexed his slender biceps, which insisted on remaining slender despite his new attempts at weight lifting. "I'm withering away."

"Let's check the freezer," said Elaine. "Maybe there's something Mom overlooked. Excuse me," she said, reaching past him to open the freezer side of the refrigerator. She brushed against Carl sort of accidentally-on-purpose, hoping he'd get the idea she was in the mood for more than food.

"Ah-ha, some forgotten goodies," said Carl, totally oblivious of her body so close to his. "Got any root beer?" he asked, pulling out a bunch of different ice cream containers.

"Here you go," said Elaine, digging some diet root beer out from under the counter. Carl began constructing a root beer float with the same intensity and precision he'd use to program a computer, dissect a frog, or mix volatile chemicals. Carl was intense, all right, but only about one thing at a time.

4

Elaine leaned against the counter, watching. Her new perfume hadn't worked. Nor had the peach-colored cotton blouse Karen had helped her sew, the one they'd cut super low in back. "To show off your best feature," Karen had joked. Unfortunately, she'd been right.

Elaine slipped off her shoes, trying to increase the one-inch difference between her and Carl. Going barefoot was one of the tricks she'd learned early in life when she realized she was going to be a giant. She'd gone through her first year of high school with her shoulders hunched over, in a desperate attempt to look shorter. That stopped, suddenly, the day she'd caught sight of herself in the mirror outside Macy's. "I looked like the hunchback of Glenwood High," she'd told her friends. Luckily, Elaine finally stopped growing when she hit five feet nine.

"Boy," she said, lifting her hair seductively off her neck, trying hard to sound sexy, "it's sure quiet in the house when everyone's asleep."

"That's for sure," said Carl, licking a drip of ice cream off the side of his glass. "It's amazing how much noise eight-year-old twins and a fourteen-year-old can make."

"Isn't it, though," said Elaine, letting her hair drop back down. Taking off her eyeglasses used to be her signal to Carl that she was ready for kissing. Why had she thought contact lenses were so great? *Now* how was she supposed to let him know? Carl seemed to need a signal, and

Elaine was too timid to come right out and say something. Dead end. Impasse. Dreamily, Elaine picked up a spoon and started scooping ice cream into a glass.

Why was she feeling so totally blah? After all, it wasn't as if her romance with Carl had ever been red hot. It was more like lukewarm, based mainly on friendship and mutual respect. Of course, that had been just fine when they'd started out. Back then, an aggressive boy would have sent her running in the opposite direction.

Elaine sneaked a glance at Carl, whose head bobbed studiously over his ice cream creation. Under that untamable sandy brown hair and fine dry wit lurked one of the brightest minds at Glenwood High. Actually, Carl was a perfect first boyfriend. He was kind and gentle and considerate. Elaine knew *she* was the one who was changing, not Carl. She was coming out of her shell and was ready for some heavy-duty romance in her life. *Am I wrong to want to be swept off my feet?* she wondered. *Is it asking too much to hear someone whisper sweet nothings in my ear?*

"...and, with this new process," Carl was saying, "I can make a printed picture of you from one of your old home videos. I'll be able to reproduce a single frozen frame of videotape onto my computer printer."

Elaine smiled and nodded. Well, so much for sweet nothings, she thought. Maybe that was their problem: their relationship was stuck in a freeze frame and she was ready for a moving picture. Carl wanted to put Elaine's face on a computer printer. Zack was the type to star her in an entire movie.

Did every thought have to involve films just because Zack was studying filmmaking? Elaine knew it wasn't fair to compare Carl to Zack. She hardly knew Zack. Not face-to-face, anyway. Their relationship—if that's what she could call it—was taking place during his nightly phone calls. Elaine had barely laid eyes on him since that first time they'd met at Karen's house.

"Interesting."

Carl's amused voice broke into Elaine's fantasy. She followed his gaze to the counter, dismayed to find she'd been scooping orange sherbet instead of vanilla ice cream into her float.

"That looks majorly disgusting," said Carl, who was very particular about his food. He took his float to the table.

"It's innovative," said Elaine, secretly agreeing with Carl. She sat across from him. "I'm tired of the same old thing all the time. Don't you ever want to try something new and different? Take a wild chance?"

"Parachute out of a moving plane, yes. Grab a shuttle into space, sure. But putting orange sherbet in a root beer float is a little too wild for me," he said. "If you ask me, you're showing all the classic signs of spring fever. Your mind is wandering, you are eating very strange food combinations..."

As Carl launched into a scientific report on the physiological changes brought on by spring, Elaine miserably forced herself to eat her orange sherbet root beer float. "Prime candidates for spring fever," Carl said, "are slender, nervous, shy people, under age twenty. Blood acidity changes during April, and that's one of the factors that determines how you feel."

"You don't seem to have 'spring fever,'" Elaine said. "And you're slender and under twenty."

"I'm not nervous or shy."

"Oh, and I suppose I am?"

Carl shrugged. "If the symptoms fit..."

"Maybe you're right." Elaine sighed, taking her empty glass to the sink. "Spring fever would sure explain things."

Carl came up next to her, standing close as he cleaned his glass and set it next to hers on the counter. What a waste, she thought. Mom and Dad and the girls were asleep. She and Carl had the whole downstairs to themselves. And nothing, absolutely *nothing* was happening.

"Elaine?" Carl took her hand in his. Had he read her mind?

"Yes?" She swallowed nervously, aware of the firmness of his grip, the warmth of his hand. Wanting romance was one thing. The prospect

8

of having it was another, altogether.

"I'm sorry if I've seemed a little, well, distracted lately. I didn't want to say anything until I knew for sure. I was afraid I'd jinx myself."

"Say anything about what?" asked Elaine. He looked so serious. "Is something wrong?"

"No, nothing like that. It's just that I've made an application for a summer internship at three different computer companies in Silicon Valley."

"Carl, that's wonderful!"

"Not so far," he said sadly. "I mean, nothing's happened yet. One company rejected me outright. They already have all their interns. But I still have a chance at Apple and IBM. I have appointments with each to go in and design a program to their specifications. Sort of like an audition."

"That should be easy for you," said Elaine, squeezing his hand reassuringly. "You're always designing programs for the teachers at school. You did that Spanish spelling quiz for Señora Kogan, and the calculus program..."

"But, don't you see, that was high school stuff. In the valley I'll be up against some of the best computer brains in California. I...I only mentioned it because I know I haven't been myself lately, and I didn't want you to think it was because of something you'd done."

So *that's* why he'd been so unresponsive to her attempts to interest him. "To tell the truth," comforted Elaine, "I hadn't noticed. I guess I've had a few things on my mind, too."

"You know," said Carl, smiling secretively, "I think I have just the cure for what ails both of us." He slipped his arm around Elaine, his hand resting lightly on the bare skin of her back as he led her into the den.

At last! thought Elaine, tingling to the warmth of his hand, her heartbeat racing in anticipation. How could she have thought Carl unromantic? He just had something important on his mind. Poor Carl. Elaine had been so busy feeling sorry for herself, she hadn't even noticed how unhappy he was. Carl could probably be as romantic as any other boy. All he needed was a little prodding, a little suggesting, a little time.

"Some boys need pushing in the romance department," her friend Alex Enomoto had told her. Alex's first boyfriend, Danny, had been a lot like Carl. Of course, Elaine thought Alex's last boyfriend, Wes the race car driver, seemed too fast in everything he did. Elaine didn't feel quite ready for someone like him.

"There's nothing wrong with the girl taking the initiative once in a while," her sexy friend Kit had told her. "Usually, if you're standing around wishing a boy would kiss you, he's probably standing around wishing you'd do the same thing to him." Of course, Kit seemed to draw boys like a perfectly proportioned magnet, and Elaine doubted Kit's advice would work for every girl. Not that Elaine was unattractive. Especially not since her friend Lori had helped make her over. Lori called it Project Super Brain to Super Beauty. Maybe Super Beauty was stretching things a bit, but there was no doubt Elaine's makeover had been a fabulous success.

"Come into my parlor," said Carl, drawing Elaine down next to him on the big overstuffed couch, "said the spider to the fly." He draped his arm over her shoulders and Elaine tingled in anticipation of his kiss. Once again she closed her eyes and tilted her head back, her lips ready for the warmth of his.

"Reach for the sky!" blared a voice.

Elaine jumped, staring wide-eyed as a cowboy movie came into focus on the TV screen. Carl stared at the screen, adjusting the volume with the remote control.

"One of the first Lash LaRue westerns," he said excitedly. "They're having a one-month LaRue festival. I've already sent in fifteen postcards to try and win one of the six-foot bullwhips they're giving out. One for each night of the festival. They'll have the drawing at midnight."

Elaine narrowed her eyes, glaring angrily at Carl. In the last minute he'd shown more interest and enthusiasm about a cowboy and a bullwhip than he had toward her all night. She moved away, curling up in the far corner of the couch.

"Is something wrong?" asked Carl, puzzled. "You look a little annoyed."

"It's nothing," said Elaine. "Just some of that old spring fever, I guess."

She stared glumly at the screen. A bank robber tried running from Lash LaRue. The handsome black-clad hero uncoiled his bullwhip and, with a flick of his wrist, sent the leather lash coiling like a python around the villain's body. The villain twisted and struggled but couldn't free himself. *That's just how I feel,* Elaine thought miserably, *bound and trapped and going nowhere.*

Saturday night, near the witching hour.
Waiting for the bathtub to fill.

Dear Journal,
  First of all, you are not dear.
  Second you are not my idea. I've never kept a journal. If I had kept one, I would have written with an elegant plumed quill instead of a Bic medium ballpoint. And my journal would have been a silk-bound book with handmade paper and a solid gold lock instead of this seasick-green wide-ruled spiral notebook.
  But yesterday Mrs. Kamala informed us that anyone who intends to get an A in her Advanced Placement English class must keep a daily journal for the rest of the school year

and must use this particular kind of book. She said she won't read our journals (we'll see about that), but she will check our books each Monday for entries. This is my first.

Mrs. Kamala doesn't care what we say or how long it takes us to say it. Which is good. My bath is almost ready, and I'm tired from my date, and I think journals are dumb. A's in English, however, are not.

Elaine

Chapter Two

She lay back, breathing out slowly through her mouth, sinking down, down into the steaming water. The big claw-foot bathtub was one of Elaine's favorite places in the Gregorys' old Victorian house. She sighed, sinking totally under the water.

She'd finally sent Carl home after a half hour of Lash LaRue and late-night commercials. Carl's attention had seemed to be focused on everything but romance, caught somewhere between cowboy bull whips and silicon computer chips. At first, Elaine had been afraid Carl would be upset when she'd said she was tired. How relieved she'd been when Carl seemed perfectly content to leave.

Now, drifting in the water scented with White

Shoulders perfume, bobbing up and down like a cork as she breathed in and out, Elaine's mind floated pleasantly, random thoughts connecting like fragile strands of a web. *Charlotte's Web*, she thought, picturing the delightful book she'd been reading the twins at night. They loved the spider who spelled messages in her web. ZACK. ZACK. Elaine smiled, picturing Charlotte's web with ZACK spun in the center.

The phone! Zack!!

Elaine shot up out of the tub, threw a towel around herself, yanked open the door, and dove for the telephone as the second ring sounded softly in the upstairs hallway.

"Hi," she whispered, breathlessly, "hold on."

She unraveled the long cord, and her wet feet slapped against the pine floor planks as she raced down the hall and up the stairs to the privacy of her attic bedroom. It had been Carl who had rigged the extra-long cord so their late-night calls wouldn't disturb Elaine's sleeping family. Funny, she couldn't remember the last time Carl had called at night. At least, she thought as she closed her bedroom door, the cord was being put to good use again.

"Okay," she said, wondering if her voice betrayed her excitement.

"How did you know it was me?" Zack's husky voice sent shivers playing tag through her body. "I know! You have one of those futuristic videophones. You're looking at me right now. Well, I can see you, too. Mmmmm, not bad."

Elaine's face grew hot as she pulled her towel more tightly around her. She pressed the phone hard against her ear, as if that would bring Zack closer to her. She paced the room nervously, holding the phone in one hand and the receiver in the other. She could almost feel him with her, imagine his strong muscled arms around her. How she wished he was there with her. How she would *die* if he actually were!

"I knew it was you," she said, trying to keep her voice light and casual, "because no one else I know calls after midnight."

"Is it that late?" He sounded contrite. "Nah. I can't believe it! Boy, time flies when you're being tortured."

Elaine laughed. Zack even *sounded* like Bill Murray. "Where are you?"

"Just came home. I've spent what could have been a beautiful night chained to an editing machine in Columbia College's film department."

"That sounds painful." She could see his blue eyes sparkling as he talked.

"Excruciating. But it's the only way I'll finish my entry for next week's film festival."

"You have to finish a movie by next *week*?!"

"Don't get upset. I do my best work under pressure."

"You do?"

"You mean I don't? Actually I don't know. I've

never done an assignment ahead of time in my life. I tend to procrastinate. I was going to join Procrastinators of America, but I haven't gotten around to it yet. Hang on."

There was a rustling sound and the creak of springs. Elaine pictured Zack stretching out on his bed. She became aware that her jaws ached from smiling. Why did she feel so happy when she talked to him?

"Ahhh," he said, "that's better. Well, now that we both know how I've wasted a perfectly good Saturday night, why don't you tell me what a gorgeous girl like you is doing home so early."

"Oh, well, Carl and I decided to spend the night here." Elaine detailed her evening with Carl, trying to make it sound as exciting as possible. After all, the one time Zack had asked her out, she'd made very sure he understood she was going with Carl. She wanted Zack to understand she wasn't the type to sneak around behind her boyfriend's back. Zack had said he respected that. Still, he'd started calling her every night, "just to keep in touch."

"Sounds like a fascinating evening," Zack said, yawning loudly. "I don't play cards, especially not bridge. And I'm not much of a cowboy fan. Although, I think *The Great Train Robbery* was the most innovative film in the early days of filmmaking."

Elaine flopped onto her bed, listening to the excitement build into Zack's voice as he talked about movies. It was the way Carl's voice sounded when he discussed computers. The big difference was, although Elaine was interested in computers, she was *passionate* about movies. Zack's conversations fascinated her.

Lying back on her bed, eyes closed, listening to Zack detail the historical cinematic importance of *The Great Train Robbery*, Elaine felt the same electricity she'd felt the first time she met Zack at Karen's house. Elaine and Karen had been watching an old Hitchcock movie on the VCR when Zack walked in and started a conversation about movies.

"Did you know," he'd said, barely looking at Elaine, "that in *Psycho*, Hitchcock never showed the knife and the woman in the shower in the same frame? Yet, through brilliant editing, the audience was made to believe it had witnessed a horribly bloody murder."

"Yes," Elaine had said, caught up in one of her favorite subjects, "and he used chocolate for the blood in the shower scene." *That* had gotten Zack's attention. He tilted his head, looking at her curiously.

"And stand-ins for both Janet Leigh and Anthony Perkins," said Zack.

"Yes. Perkins was in New York rehearsing a play."

Zack sat next to her on the sofa, regarding Elaine closely, as if seeing her—really seeing her—for the first time. She felt suddenly self-conscious being the object of his obvious attention.

"It took a week to shoot..."

"...that one minute of final footage," Elaine finished.

Zack had run his hand through his thick, unruly hair.

"A movie trivia duel." Karen laughed delightedly. "Zack, my good man, I do believe you've met your match!"

"And she was stabbed..."

"Fourteen times!" said Elaine.

Karen's red curls bounced as her head bobbed from side to side, following their exchange like a spectator at a tennis match.

"Hitchcock had seventy-eight different editing cuts in one minute," Zack had said.

"Oh, no. There were seventy-nine setups," corrected Elaine.

"Seventy-eight," Zack had said.

"Seventy-nine."

They had gone, arguing, to his bedroom, where he kept his extensive library of film books. By the time they found the correct answer—seventy-eight—Elaine felt there was enough electricity flowing between them to power a small town. When, on the spur of the moment, Zack asked Elaine to an Ingmar Bergman festival on campus, it had taken every iota of her willpower to say no. She told Zack about Carl as quickly as she could, before her defenses weakened any more than they already had.

"So"—the hoarseness in Zack's voice reflected his weariness from a long day of editing—"I'd really like to borrow you next Saturday night."

"Borrow me?"

"Well, I know all about you and Carl, and I don't want to step on any toes. But our student film festival is next weekend, and I'll be showing my first movie. Since you're the only person I know who's nearly as knowledgeable as I am about films . . ."

"Nearly?"

". . . it would mean a lot to me if you'd come. I don't know why, but I respect your taste. I'd like to borrow you, to get your opinion. I promise to give you back to Carl after the showing."

"It sounds exciting," said Elaine.

"What does? Being given back to Carl?"

She laughed. "The movie festival. But . . ."

"No 'buts,'" said Zack. "Look, I'm not asking you out on a date. I'm only borrowing you for one teeny tiny evening. Can't you set Carl in front of a Lash LaRue movie and tell him you'll be right back?"

"It *would* be fascinating," said Elaine.

"What would? Leaving Carl in front of a Lash LaRue movie?"

"Zack Waverly!" Elaine laughed. "Aren't you ever serious?"

"I am always serious. Will you marry me?"

"Zack, you're getting punchy. Go to sleep." Elaine wished she could see Zack's face. She had a good imagination, but she wanted the real thing.

"Not until you promise to come to the festival."

Elaine desperately wanted to go. But how could she accept without feeling disloyal to Carl. Of course, Zack was only "borrowing" her for an evening. It wasn't like a date. Zack was a friend. Don't make more out of this than it is, Elaine told herself.

"Is Karen going?" she asked.

"Would my little sister pass up a chance to see me make a fool of myself?"

"I...I guess I could go with Karen," said Elaine.

"Is that a yes?"

"I guess, if I can get a ride with Karen..."

"You've got it! Great! Now will you hang up this phone so I can get some sleep? I swear I don't know why I hang around with people who call at all hours of the night!"

"'Night, Zack," Elaine said.

"'Night."

Elaine held the phone to her ear long after Zack had hung up.

Lying on her bed, looking up through her skylight, Elaine tried to sort out the crazy quilt of emotions rushing in on her.

Guilt. She couldn't be disloyal to Carl. He was too dear to her. Hurting him would be the last thing she would want. Especially now, when he was so worried about that internship in Silicon Valley and needed her support more than ever.

Desire. There was no denying the powerful attraction she felt for Zack. His humor, his interests, everything about Zack Waverly fascinated and delighted her. Thoughts of him were never far from her mind.

Fear. Was Zack *too* attractive? Hadn't Elaine learned her lesson the time she fell for heartthrob football star Rusty Hughes? She'd learned then that looks weren't everything.

In fact, she thought sadly, looks weren't anything...but trouble. It seemed people who'd been attractive all their lives never had to work as hard to develop inner strength and character as people who blossomed late—like Elaine, who'd only recently metamorphosed from moth to butterfly.

Sure it was fun to fantasize about falling in love with someone as exciting as Zack. Elaine would have to be made of stone not to be affected by his aura of sensitivity, sensuality, and romance. But her own painful past experience warned her some types of love were like riding a bullet train without brakes. Elaine wasn't at all sure the thrill of the ride was worth the crash at the end.

Saturday, one-ish, can't sleep.
In kitchen eating slices of tomatoes and cukes
on whole wheat bread. Mint tea.

Dear Journal,
    P.S. Just thought I should mention that a
certain Zachary Waverly called. (After all,
Mrs. Kamala says a journal will one day help
us remember when events happened in our
lives. Not that Zachary Waverly's call is an
"event." Not exactly. He calls quite often to
chat. Love that word. Chat. So frightfully
proper. Chit-chat and all that.)
    Zack is quite interested in my knowledge of
the film industry. He is studying filmmaking
at Columbia and has asked me to come to the

film festival next week. I am honored that he asked, although I am not certain I can work the festival into my plans. I told him I'd try and come. I hate to turn down a friend's request. Still, if Carl has already made plans for us to do something next weekend, I will really have to refuse Zack's invitation.

I wonder if this can count as a separate journal entry. Even if it's made on the same day as the last one. I don't see why not. But Mrs. Kamala might have an objection. Maybe I should date this entry Sunday. Hey! It is Sunday. Barely. But who cares?

Think I'm finally tired enough to sleep. Journal writing, the sleep aid of the eighties. Maybe you're not such a bad idea after all. I'll see. 'Nite.

Elaine the Movie Buff

Chapter Three

As usual, Elaine was the last one in her family to arrive at the breakfast table. Easing into the chair next to her father, she stared at the cool waffle waiting for her on her plate.

"Why didn't you two have some waffles with your syrup?" Mr. Gregory was saying, futilely trying to coax the few last drops from the maple syrup bottle.

"Oh, Daddy," said Chrissie, stuffing a huge piece of syrup-soaked waffle into her mouth.

"Oh, Daddy," echoed her eight-year-old twin, Carla.

Elaine poured a large glass of orange juice from the pitcher and listened quietly. Unlike the rest of her family, she was not a "morning person," usually not really waking up until she

27

got off the bus at school.

"Your teeth are going to rot and fall out of your mouths," warned Andrea, sounding more like the twins' mother than their fourteen-year-old sister.

"More teeth out, more money in," said Chrissie matter-of-factly.

"I *looooove* the tooth fairy!" said Carla. She smiled sideways to show the new space where four frantically chewed pieces of bubble gum had helped one of her baby teeth "fall" out.

Elaine reached for the powdered sugar, shaking it like snow on her waffle.

"Well," Andrea cautioned the twins, "you'll look mighty dumb on dates, having to gum your food to death."

"Not dating yet," said Chrissie, pushing in another mouthful. "Besides, the way you eat takes too long."

"Filling each little waffle hole with one drop of syrup." Carla wrinkled her nose. "Yuck."

"Preparing food slowly and eating slowly are weight-loss tricks," said Andrea, neatly cutting her half waffle into tiny pieces.

"We don't need to lose weight," said Chrissie.

"Not *yet*," said Andrea, raising a disapproving eyebrow at the sea of syrup on the twins' plates. "But some of us do. I, for one, am determined to find out if there are cheekbones lurking under these fat cheeks."

"Since when are waffles a diet food?" asked

Elaine.

"It's too hard to give up my favorite foods," explained Andrea. "So I'm cutting each of my usual portions in half and saving the other half for another meal. So far I've lost twelve pounds. Just another three hundred to go."

Elaine laughed. "Good for you," she said, delighted to see Andrea finally approaching her excess weight with humor rather than depression. "Keep up whatever you're doing. You look wonderful! Have the kids at school noticed?"

"Well, yesterday Steve Bennett, who is a notch above gorgeous, asked if I was doing my hair a new way or something."

She's primed and ready, thought Elaine, now all she needs is the right boy to notice her. Elaine remembered how she'd felt when her entire world hovered expectantly on the edge of dating. Of course, Andrea was so much more sophisticated. At fourteen, Elaine had been as skinny and gawky as Andrea was plump and graceful. Elaine never had someone like Steve Bennett say anything *remotely* complimentary to her.

The trouble with being the oldest was not having someone to break ground for you. No one to mimic. No one to teach you how to dress or flirt or put on makeup. Which was probably why such things were recent developments in Elaine's life. Andrea, on the other hand, watched Elaine constantly, asking millions of

29

questions, many of them extremely personal. *Why couldn't I have had an older sister,* thought Elaine wistfully. *Maybe by now I'd have gone through a hundred boys instead of still being with my first.*

"Gotta get going," said Elaine, trying to gulp down the last few bites of waffle before heading off to school.

"Just wait one second, honey," said Mrs. Gregory, coming to the table. She sat playfully on Mr. Gregory's lap.

"Dad and I have a little something to tell you girls." She ruffled Mr. Gregory's thinning blond hair. "You want to tell them, or should I?"

"I'll flip you for it," he said, putting his arms around her and squeezing her gently.

Andrea looked away, embarrassed. Poor kid, thought Elaine, remembering how awkward she used to feel when her parents became playful. Somehow, as Elaine grew older, she began to consider their affection toward each other natural and wonderful.

"No flipping," warned Mrs. Gregory. "Well, girls, it looks like the garage sale we had when Dad was out of work wasn't such a great idea, after all."

"But, we made lots of money," said Chrissie.

"And we didn't need any of that old stuff," said Carla.

"I think we'll be needing some of that 'old stuff' pretty soon," said Mrs. Gregory.

"Yup," said Mr. Gregory, "like the baby buggy, the crib, the bassinet, the..."

"Mom!" Andrea gasped. "You're not...you can't..."

"I am." Mrs. Gregory beamed.

"She can," said Mr. Gregory.

Elaine felt the last bite of waffle go down the wrong way, choking her, sending her into a fit of coughing.

"Elaine!" Her mother jumped up and hit her firmly on the back. Elaine couldn't get her breath. The waffle was blocking her air passage. Panic gripped her.

"Stand back," ordered Mr. Gregory. He grabbed Elaine from behind, jerking his clenched fists hard under Elaine's ribs in the Heimlich maneuver. A small piece of waffle popped out. Elaine dragged air deeply into her lungs.

"Here, honey," her mom said, handing her a glass of water.

"Thanks," coughed Elaine, sitting down and sipping the water slowly.

The twins, always the first to recover from disaster, chattered happily about what it was going to be like having a new baby in the house.

"At least *we* won't be the babies around here anymore," said Chrissie.

"Will you excuse me, please," said Andrea, rushing red faced from the kitchen.

Elaine sat numbly, listening as the twins and

her parents babbled about the new baby. How could her parents do this? It was absolutely crazy! With four children already, what could they possibly want with a fifth? Especially since the family was only now beginning to recover from the hard times they'd suffered when her father was out of work.

For her parents' sake, Elaine forced herself to seem happy.

"That's great news," she said, kissing them both before going upstairs to get ready for school. As she passed the second-floor bathroom, Andrea rushed out, her eyes red from crying.

"Andrea, what is it?" asked Elaine, putting a comforting hand on Andrea's shoulder.

"How could they?" Andrea said angrily. "At their age! When Mom starts to show, everyone will know they . . . well, you know."

"Yes, I know," said Elaine, hugging Andrea, suppressing a smile. "I understand."

"You can't."

"Of course I can. You know my friend Kit's mom?"

"Sure. Mrs. McCoy's almost as beautiful as Kit. I remember the first time I saw her I thought she was Kit's sister."

"That's her, all right. Now, don't repeat this . . ."

"Cross my heart."

" . . . when I was fourteen, Kit told me about

her mother's newest boyfriend. He'd started sleeping over at their apartment."

"That's awful!"

"I was so embarrassed for Kit. I'd said I was glad my mom had finished having children so she didn't have to think about sex anymore. I mean, it never occurred to me our parents still 'did it.' Talk about naive!"

"I'm not that bad," said Andrea, managing a small laugh. "I figured they—you know—when they went away on vacation. But, with Dad losing his job and then starting a new one, Mom and Dad haven't gone anywhere. That means they were home when...when they...It's so embarrassing!"

"Tell me about it," Elaine sympathized. "Kit and Alex couldn't stop laughing at me. It took them all of three seconds to set me straight. Of course, I couldn't look at Mom and Dad for *weeks* after that. At night I'd strain to listen to see if I could hear anything. On television, couples making love are very noisy. The trouble was, in this old creaky Victorian house, there were a zillion night noises. After a while, I gave up. I figured if Mom and Dad were still fooling around, it was their business." She looked into Andrea's eyes. "Does that make sense to you?"

"I guess so," said Andrea, brushing wisps of fine blond hair back off her face. "But it's going to take some getting used to. I wonder what my friends are going to say about Mom being pregnant?"

"They'll take their cue from you," said Elaine, following Andrea into her poster-covered bedroom. "You know how crazy your friend Posey Tillman gets when her mother goes out on a date?"

"She hates it!" said Andrea, fishing two matching socks from a pile on the floor. "She thinks it's horrible for her mother to date. One night she saw her mother kiss a man in their living room, and she went crazy."

"I know. I remember hearing you on the phone, sympathizing with her. But her mother's only thirty-seven years old. She's hardly ready for an old people's home. She should be dating and enjoying life."

Andrea nodded agreement. "Actually, I feel sort of sorry for Mrs. Tillman. Posey told me she makes a scene every time her mom tries to bring a man into the house."

"Wouldn't it be easier for everyone if Posey were more understanding? Like Kit. She treats her mother's dating so casually that I don't think anything about it. If you're happy about Mom's pregnancy, your friends will think it's great. If you're angry and walk around sulking, they'll think it's awful."

"I guess that's why they're my friends."

"I guess."

Andrea hugged Elaine. "Thanks."

"Anytime," said Elaine, hugging her back.

"Now, we'd better hurry or we'll be late for school."

Elaine ran up to her attic room to dab on eye shadow, mascara, and lipstick. The face staring back from the mirror wasn't entirely happy. She'd put up a good front for Andrea's sake, but she wasn't feeling all that noble.

Munchkin, the Siamese kitten Carl had given her as a gift after her tomcat, Bessie, had been killed, had settled on top of her makeup case. Gently she lifted him off and set him next to it on the dresser top.

"As a matter of fact," Elaine said, slipping on a headband to hold back her hair, "you feel pretty miserable. Don't you?" She tilted her head back, brushing mascara on her upper lashes. "Just when the twins are getting fairly independent, you're going to be stuck baby-sitting all over again." She tilted her head down, darkening her lower lashes.

"It's even worse now," she explained to Munchkin as she outlined her lips with Perfectly Plum, filling them in with Rapturous Rose. "Andrea can help with the sitting, but I'm the only child who drives. Three guesses who'll be doing grocery shopping, running errands..." Elaine put her hands on her dresser and leaned into the mirror, her golden brown eyes looking sadly back at her. "Your parents have no right to do this to you," she said, but her voice and words lacked conviction. Elaine was part of a family, and that meant sharing responsibilities.

Sinking onto her bed to slip on her sandals, she knew what was *really* bothering her: she was going to have to watch her mother growing bigger and bigger every day. Home used to be Elaine's haven from the outside world. Now, everywhere Elaine turned, she would be reminded of sex.

Munchkin jumped from the dresser onto the bed. Elaine stroked his soft fur. "And thinking of sex is just what I *don't* need," she said. Especially not now when thoughts of Zack were beginning to intrude on everything she did... when powerful, strange yearnings were awakening in her body.

Monday, 5:03 P.M.
In the car picking up twins.
Light drizzle. Roads really slick. Whoopee!
Ain't driving fun?

Dear Journal,
I'm sitting here waiting for Chrissie, so I might as well write in you and get it over with.

Mrs. Kamala did not—repeat—did not look at what any of us had written. She just checked to see there was something in our journals. A couple of my classmates were upset. They'd made up some really raunchy stuff, hoping she'd read it. No such luck.

After class I was in the washroom and heard Cherish Lynch reading her entries to a group of her friends. We were sure in the right room for what she'd written. Look out, Jackie Collins! Here comes Cherish. Her entries were so hot they scorched the pages. Smokin'!

Ho-hum. Chrissie's still inside her friend's house searching for her shoes. Carla's here in the back seat with my colored felt-tip pens drawing moustaches on the faces in my history book. It was the only way I could think of to calm her down. This was the twins' first time at their new friend's home, and it turns out the mom is a screamer. Carla got so scared she'd cried and wouldn't stop until I came to get her.

"What did she scream about?" I asked Carla.

"Everything."

"Like?"

"Don't play in the living room!" She screeched like her friend's mother. Carla's a great mimic. "Don't take your juice out of the kitchen. Don't tease the bird. Don't turn on the TV. Why can't you play like young ladies instead of wild savages?"

"Some kids have all the luck," I said. "Why can't our mom yell like that?"

That got a little smile out of Carla. Poor kid.

What makes some people yell all the time? I hear women in the grocery store screaming at cute little kids. Mom says people who are always yelling feel there's no one in their lives

38

listening to them. It's sure true at school. The kids who make trouble in class seem hungry for attention. It's annoying and it's sad and I'm glad I don't live in a yelling-type house. Of course, Chrissie and Carla make their share of noise. In fact, Carla makes so much racket of her own I don't know why she can't stand someone else's. Maybe Mom should yell every once in a while to get the twins used to it.

Which reminds me, guess whose mother is P.G.?

Eating for two?

Has a bun in the oven?

Right. And guess which daughter will be doing more errands than ever? Right again. Like now. Here I am sitting and waiting for the twins when I have tons of other things I should be doing. Junior year I read a book called Been Down So Long It Looks Like Up to Me. I'm beginning to think I could have written it.

Carla just showed me her artwork. You know, Cleopatra doesn't look half bad with a green beard and purple moustache. Wonder if Antony would have liked her that way?

Here comes Chrissie. Bye.

Elaine the Chauffeur

Chapter Four

"No, no, stand back! Wait for the ball to come to you. Back. Back." Karen, a blur of red hair and motion, yelled instructions to Elaine across the Ping-Pong table. "That's it. That's it!"

The girls concentrated intensely. The musty basement was silent except for the click of the white ball on the green table. Elaine drew Karen off-balance, lifted her paddle, moved in for the kill, and...

"Aren't you two *ever* going to be done?"

...missed! Whirling toward the basement stairs, Elaine glared crossly at Carla and Chrissie, who had come down for what seemed the millionth time.

"How come you two never want to play Ping-Pong except when I'm playing?" snapped

Elaine.

"We forget about it," explained Carla.

"Until we hear you playing," said Chrissie.

"You can't fight logic like that," said Karen.

"Well, we're still not done," said Elaine. "So scat!"

The twins scampered cheerfully back up the stairs, leaving Elaine and Karen alone.

"Couldn't you become interested in a non-Ping-Pong player?" asked Elaine.

"Elaine Gregory! Whatever do you mean? I am simply trying out for the Ping-Pong team."

"Which just happens to have a gorgeous captain."

"I already have a boyfriend, thank you very much. Your serve."

"Do you mean to stand there and tell me you are practicing Ping-Pong because you love the game?" Elaine smashed the ball across the net, missing the table completely.

Karen laughed, holding up her hands in surrender. "Welllll, *maybe* I *might* have noticed Terry Conrad was *marginally* attractive."

"Then why not just go up to him and say, 'Hi, I find you marginally attractive' without going through all this?"

"I *always* immerse myself in whatever interests a boy who interests me." Karen put down her paddle, readjusting the two hair combs holding back the sides of her frizzy red hair. "Among other things, I've become an expert on

Shakespeare, drag racing, opera, short-order cooking, car repair, and yoga."

"Sounds confusing," said Elaine, serving more gently. They volleyed easily. "With Carl, all I need to know about is computers. What are Jeff's interests?"

"Ahhhh," swooned Karen, "Jeff Becker has devoted his life to the search for the ultimate chocolate chip cookie."

"Now there's an interest I can relate to," said Elaine.

"And I don't want you to think I'm not crazy about Jeff. It's just that, since we spend half our time wisecracking and trading insults, I want to have someone primed and ready when we break up for the nine thousand nine hundred and ninety-ninth time. I figure it won't hurt to brush up my Ping-Pong game, just in case."

How well Elaine understood. Learning more about a boy's interests was exactly why she'd been brushing up on her movie trivia, memorizing as many facts as possible so she'd be able to match wits with Zack. Elaine longed to tell Karen about her feelings for Zack. But what if she did, and Karen told her brother? No, she thought, watching Karen chase a missed ball under the sofa. As close as Elaine felt to Karen, she knew the bond between brother and sister was stronger. Elaine couldn't risk having Zack know her feelings. She felt safe talking to him on the phone at night, but what if he came after her in person? Would she have the strength to turn him away the way she did that night in his room when he'd asked her out? Probably not. And there was no way Elaine could justify leading Zack on while she was still attached to Carl.

"You seem upset," Karen said, looking thoughtfully at Elaine. Elaine smashed the Ping-Pong ball so hard it hit the far wall. She couldn't talk to Karen about Zack, but she could share her other problems.

"My mother's going to have a baby," said Elaine unhappily.

"But, that's wonderful!" said Karen.

"You say that because you're the baby in your family. All you have to do is be cute."

"Do my best," said Karen, comically blowing out her cheeks and crossing her eyes.

Elaine set her paddle on the table and sank into the old musty-smelling couch. "It gets pretty rough being the oldest," she said. "I'm already handling about as much as I can, between school, work, and home. The new baby is going to add to the long list of things I'm responsible for."

Karen sat beside Elaine. "I nearly wasn't the baby in my family," she said, her usually happy face clouding. "When I was ten years old, my mother got pregnant. I was so jealous...resentful. I had been my family's little girl for so long that I didn't want to give up my place. And I knew, from friends who had younger brothers and sisters, I would have to take care of the baby. I remember thinking, 'When I want to take care of kids, I'll have my own.' I hated the idea of being tied down."

Elaine had never seen Karen this serious. She felt a bond forming between them, the kind of bond that leads to intense friendships, like those she shared with Kit, Alex, and Lori.

Karen picked at a loose thread on the sofa. "I didn't have to worry. My mom had a miscarriage." Her perpetually bubbly voice was barely a whisper. "I blamed myself for the miscarriage. I was sure my hateful thoughts caused it."

"But, that's silly," comforted Elaine. "Thinking things—good or bad—can't make them come true."

"I know that now. But, when you're ten, you think the world revolves around you. It wasn't until I was a few years older that I understood the only thing my negative thoughts caused was my own unhappiness. Eight years have passed, and sometimes I still wonder what my sister would have been like."

An unexpected tear rolled down Karen's cheek, and Elaine put a comforting arm around her. "Isn't it funny how we never really know what goes on in other people's lives?"

Karen nodded. "That's why it's so dumb to envy other people. You never can tell what heartache they've been through or what burdens they're bearing. Like when you told me

45

Alex Enomoto had lost a brother to cystic fibrosis. I could hardly believe it! You sure can't tell she's suffered a tragedy by looking at her."

"She's pretty good at hiding her feelings," said Elaine. "When Noodle died, Alex was pretty broken up. Luckily, she had people in her life she could talk to."

"My problem was I kept my feelings about my mother's miscarriage inside . . . until now."

"That's not healthy," said Elaine. "When people don't talk out their feelings, they can wind up like Russ Hanna. There wasn't a person at school who would have guessed he would commit suicide."

"I felt so bad when he died." Karen sighed. "If only he had said something—reached out. He probably didn't know how much he was liked by everyone. What a waste."

"Now?" begged Chrissie, stamping noisily down the stairs.

"Please?" Carla knelt at the top of the steps, her hands clasped pleadingly in front of her.

Elaine and Karen nodded to each other in silent agreement. "Okay, you two," said Elaine. "We give." She watched her little sisters take over the table. Karen's story about Mrs. Waverly's miscarriage had been a sobering one, and it made Elaine keenly aware of the love she felt for the twins. And for Andrea.

Still, three sisters were quite enough. What if Elaine's mom had another set of twins, a very likely possibility. Elaine's problems would multiply by two! Well, her mother was going in for ultrasound and tests to determine the fetus's health. She would know about twins soon enough.

"Want to take a walk over to Vogue Fabrics?" asked Karen. "They got in a new batch of polka-dot fabrics that I'd give anything to sink a needle into."

"Lead on, Mc Waverly," said Elaine, laughing.

"I'm so glad you're going to the film festival, said Karen, as they walked toward the mall. "Jeff falls asleep if there isn't a car chase and fight scene every three minutes. *The Terminator* was his ultimate movie and *Mad Max* runs a close second. He couldn't understand why those films didn't sweep the Academy Awards. From what Zack has told me about the students' films, I think Jeff is in for a boring evening."

"Will we be going with Zack?" Elaine asked casually, hoping Karen wouldn't notice the nervous eagerness in her voice.

"No. Zack has to go on ahead to help with last-minute details. You'll go with me and Jeff and my mom. Fred will come, too, if he doesn't have tons of homework. Which reminds me, my grandmother has a cold, which means we have an extra ticket. How about inviting Carl?"

Elaine's heart sank. In her fantasy, Saturday was to be her night with Zack. "Was it Zack's idea to invite Carl?" she asked.

"Of course not. You know as well as I do Zack's oblivious to anything but movies. I, however, am an incurable romantic, in love with lovers like you and Carl. I didn't want Carl to feel left out."

They entered at the south end of Glenwood Mall, ambling through the hurrying crowds of shoppers. "I...I haven't mentioned the festival to Carl, yet," said Elaine.

Karen's eyes widened with surprise. "Why on earth not?"

"I was feeling a little guilty about leaving him alone on a Saturday night."

"Then this is wonderful! Now you have a ticket for him."

"No!" The force of her response startled them both. "I mean, Carl hates innovative, experimental, and foreign films. Not necessarily in that order. He'd detest the film festival and make us all miserable with his funny little remarks." *And make me miserable,* she realized, *when what I really want is to be with Zack. If Carl is with me, nothing at all can happen. Not that I want anything to happen.*

Oh, be honest with yourself, she thought. Lately, you can't seem to get enough of Zack. You're becoming addicted to him. The more he calls, the more you need to hear his voice. When you're not talking to him, you're thinking about him.

"Okay," said Karen, stopping in front of Vogue's huge window, which was elegantly draped with fabulous fabrics. "Then I'll give the ticket to Silvano Bussetti."

"The new Italian exchange student?"

"Yep. He adores movies. I interviewed him for a public speaking assignment. He said I reminded him of Amy Irving. I told him he reminds me of Woody Allen."

"Karen!" Elaine winced. "Silvano is over six feet tall, blond, and built like a Greek god!"

"True. But, I figured a guy who looks like Silvano has girls falling all over him. My only chance to interest him was to use my perverse sense of humor as bait. I threw out the Woody Allen line and, luckily, he bit. He thought my comparison was so absurd, he couldn't stop laughing. Got us both kicked out of speech class. We went to the quad, where I watched him hiccup for fifteen minutes." She walked into the store.

"Sounds wildly romantic," said Elaine, following her in. "But where does that leave the Ping-Pong romance? Not to mention poor Jeff."

"Oh, I'll just give Silvano the ticket and let him go by himself. But I have to cover all the bases." Karen yanked the end of a bolt of cotton gauze, unraveling several yards, which she wrapped around herself like an Indian sari. Hobbling to a full-length mirror, she spoofed several modeling poses. "After all, what happens if I concentrate all my romantic energies on Jeff and then he falls in love with a Famous Amos chocolate chip cookie baker?"

Elaine stopped her search for fabric and looked up. "Cookie baker?"

"When it comes to love, stranger things have happened." Karen flung open a bolt of polka-dotted silk and swirled the fabric around her shoulders. "Or what if Mr. Ping-Pong goes off and marries a Chinese acrobat?"

"You have some peculiar ideas," said Elaine. "Which just about match your taste in fabric."

Karen wrinkled her freckled nose at her reflection. "Needs color," she said, unrolling a bolt of red plaid. She arranged the fabric carefully over the dots. "I know my relationships aren't as steady as yours and Carl's, but you have to remember we comics are basically insecure. Oh, good, a salesperson. She waved at a distraught-looking saleswoman who was barreling down the aisle toward them.

No, thought Elaine, Karen's relationships were not like hers at all. In fact, Elaine wasn't sure what her relationship with Carl was anymore. Perhaps, she decided, it was time to find out.

Tuesday
5:30 A.M.

CRAMPS! Aaaaarrrrrgggggghhhhh!!!!!!

They woke me up at 4:00, got really bad by 4:30. I didn't think I'd make it to the kitchen. Practically crawled there. Wanted to wake Mom for help, but she needs her sleep. As for Dad and the girls, forget it. It made them crazy the few times they happened to see me like this. Usually I eat six prunes before bedtime the two days before my period. Keeps me regular, and the pain is not quite so bad. But I'm early this month. (I need a good pruning. Ha ha.)

Am on my second thermos of camomile tea,

have the heating pad turned on high, took two aspirin. Mom sometimes gives me a shot glass of evil-tasting cognac to ease the pain, but I don't think I want to go to school smelling like the morning after the night before.

I think the pain's easing. Must be if I can write in you. It's still too bad to sleep, though, and I'm glad for your company. Also, I'll get you out of the way for today.

Mom once told me that after I have a baby my menstrual cramps won't be so bad. Mmmmmmmmmm, now there's an interesting way to get rid of cramps. Actually, I think she made that up. It sounds extremely unscientific. Have to check it out with Dr. Edwards the next time I see her.

I'm downstairs in the library, curled up on the window seat cushions, wrapped in the granny quilt Grandma Anne made for me when I was born. I love it here. The room smells of polished oak and old books. It's like a scene from Little Women. I wonder which sister I'd be. I'd like to be Jo—bold and outspoken. I'm not, of course. My friend Alex Enomoto could play that part. Or Karen Waverly (Zack's sister). I wonder if everyone wants to be like someone else? Does anyone think they're fine just the way they are? Doubt it.

Mom never has menstrual pains. (Of course, just now she has no period. She says it's one of the main advantages to the nine months of pregnancy.) Maybe pain skips generations. Like red hair. (Karen, Zack's sister, has red hair.) Mom said her mother had horrible periods. Used to lie in bed moaning for a couple of days. In a way, it's probably easier for me to have the pain than for Mom to have to watch me have the pain. Like when Chrissie stepped on a bee. I went crazy until I was able to tweeze the stinger out of her little foot. My own bee stings never hurt me that much.

It was raining hard when I woke up, and I'm sort of glad I was up to see it. I like the rain. Like its sound. Like the way it makes the world smell sweet and fresh. It's stopped now, and all that's left is a thick mist. I expect the sun will burn it off by school time. Which reminds me, I'd better try to get at least an hour's sleep. French quiz today. Mon Dieu!

Elaine with Pain (in the Rain), Again

Chapter Five

Elaine hurriedly cleared her materials off the computer lab work table, setting them carefully into her class locker. Now that she was building her own computer board, the class period never seemed long enough. Since this was her last class before lunch, she often spent a few extra minutes finishing her work, sometimes even missing lunch for a particularly fascinating project. But not today.

What could Carl want? He'd sent a note before class via Lori. "Meet me on the quad for lunch." That was all it said. *No one* would be eating on the quad. The ground would still be sodden from the rain.

"You should have worn boots," Lori had laughed, reaching out to straighten Elaine's thin leather tie. "The quad's probably underwater."

"Want to swim out and join us?" teased Elaine. "I think I have a musty old tank suit in my locker."

Lori pinched her nose to ward off the imaginary smell. "Sounds intriguing," she said, her voice resonating in her tightly held nose, "but I think I'll eat my salad in the cafeteria, where it's dry. Have fun."

"You and your salads." Elaine sighed as Lori raced off to her next class. It was still almost impossible to believe Lori had been fat before she came to school at Glenwood. Lori was not only slender, she was also beautiful. Luckily, she was generous, too, and had shared her beauty expertise with Elaine. Of course, even with Lori's makeover help, Elaine still found it a struggle to "put herself together."

The quad was deserted. A few late stragglers ran toward the cafeteria, but the lush lawn, usually covered with lunching kids, was empty. It took a moment before Elaine spotted Carl all but hidden around the far side of the huge eucalyptus tree. Tiptoeing up behind him to surprise him, it was Elaine who was surprised.

Carl, his thin face bent studiously over the latest issue of *Games* magazine, sat cross-legged on a huge plastic drop cloth. Elaine recognized it from the painting being done on the west wing. On top of that he'd spread the old sheet that usually camouflaged the torn sofa in the journalism room. He'd stuck some weeds into an empty soda can as a centerpiece.

"Nice place you've got here," said Elaine.

"Hi!" said Carl cheerfully. He jumped up, draped a napkin over his arm, and bowed deeply. "Welcome to Chez Carl, Madam." He gestured to a space on the sheet.

"Ah, *merci* buckets," Elaine said grandly, plopping down. "What's the occasion?" She gasped in delight. "Carl! Did you get one of the computer internships?"

"Nothing that unimportant," he said. He sat across from her, his hazel eyes bright with pride. "You, you lucky lucky person of the female persuasion, are about to experience the Carl Schmidt solution to spring fever." He started rummaging around in a large grocery bag.

Elaine watched, delighted, as Carl pulled out gift-wrapped sandwiches, crayon-decorated cartons of cole slaw and potato salad, and a thermos and set everything out on their "picnic" cloth. Leave it to Carl to find a creative solution to a problem. It would be impossible for her not have warm feelings for Carl. He was so bright, so eager, so likable. Elaine sighed deeply. But, warm feelings weren't romantic feelings. Warm feelings were what you felt for relatives and friends. They glowed inside like gentle embers. What Elaine wanted was a bolt of lightning. She sighed again.

"There you go," said Carl, "heaving those deep sighs. That's the number-one sign of an acute case of spring fever. Good thing you're getting a dose of the Carl Schmidt cure. Turkey on rye for madam?"

"Ah, oui, merci," said Elaine, delighted with Carl's attempts to cheer her. He set a pink-bowed package in front of her with a flourish.

"And P.B. and J. for monsieur," he said, digging into the assortment of goodies and pulling out a package wrapped in the Sunday comic page.

They ate in silence, enjoying the quiet of the quad and the gentle noon breezes.

"I was turned down by IBM," Carl said softly.

Her bite of turkey sandwich stuck in Elaine's throat. She reached out and put a comforting hand on Carl's arm. "Oh, Carl, I'm so sorry."

"Their loss," he said, forcing a weak smile. "I guess I'll just have to develop something spectacular for Apple. Make those guys at IBM eat their computer chips."

"When do you audition for Apple?"

"Two weeks," said Carl.

"You'll be *great*," she said enthusiastically. "You'll beat the pants off the competition."

"That should make it interesting," he said, lifting his left eyebrow. "Especially since a third of the applicants are women."

Elaine punched his arm playfully. "Seriously," she said, "look how much creativity you brought to this lunch. I can't believe you won't create the most fabulous program they've ever seen."

Carl took Elaine's hands in his. "If only you could be one of the judges," he said wistfully. "But it helps to know there's someone in this world who believes in me...and"—his gold-flecked eyes twinkled mischievously—"who appreciates my superior talents." He dug into the bag and pulled out a foil-wrapped package. "Crepes for dessert?" he asked, unwrapping a double pack of Hostess cupcakes.

"However did you guess." Elaine laughed. Lifting off the thick frosting, she ate the cake part first.

"Don't know how you can do that," said Carl, his mouth full of frosting.

"I like to save the best for last," said Elaine.

"But I'm always afraid I'll be too full for the frosting, so I eat it first." He took a huge bite of the cupcake. "Of course, that's never happened, but you never know."

"Dr. Minkus, our pediatrician, said he can tell a baby's personality by the way it eats," said Elaine. "Chrissie was a gobbler. She ate everything all at once. Dr. Minkus said she'd attack life, be outgoing, eager for new experiences, new foods, new people."

"That's Chrissie, all right," said Carl.

"Carla would take just a teeny, tiny bit of food

in her mouth, work it around awhile, spit it out, worry it to death. Dr. Minkus said she'd hang back, watch a situation before she entered, and be fussy about her food."

"I don't know how scientific his theory is," said Carl, "but it sure worked two out of two times in your family. I'll have to ask my mom if I was like Carla. I have a feeling I'll still be fanatic about keeping my food groups separated on my plate when I'm in the old people's home. Actually, it might be fun to have a new baby around to watch . . . just to see if the theory holds up."

"Funny you should mention it," said Elaine.

The edge in her voice made Carl look up, concerned. "What's the matter?"

"My mom's pregnant."

"No! Is she very upset?"

"Upset? *She's* not upset at all. *She's* happy. *She* doesn't seem concerned that we're only just recovering from Dad's being out of work. It doesn't seem to bother her that she's already busy with four of us who need her attention."

Carl listened attentively, head tilted to one side, his face filled with sympathy and support. When Elaine had finished, a smile lifted the corners of his mouth. "Fantastic!" he said.

"The baby?"

"Don't you see? The baby is the reason you've been behaving so strangely. I didn't think spring fever was all that was bothering you, but

I couldn't think of anything else. Now that we know what the problem is, we can try to work it out."

Why did he have to be so understanding, she thought miserably. She had to let Carl believe the baby was the entire reason for her touchiness. His concern made Elaine feel doubly guilty for having accepted Zack's invitation to the film festival. Zack's just a friend, she tried to tell herself. Yet, she knew in her heart the right thing to do would be to cancel out.

The quad came alive with students wandering out from the cafeteria to catch some sun, socialize, play Frisbee. Karen, Alex, Kit, and Lori came over and settled themselves down in the middle of Elaine and Carl's picnic.

"Got something for you," Karen said to Elaine. She dug into her huge shoulder bag and pulled out a packet of photos. "Delta Discount's giving two prints of every picture"—she shuffled through the large stack—"and . . . here!"

Everyone gathered around the photo of Elaine and Karen studying at Karen's house. Karen's brother Fred had captured them sprawled amid bowls of popcorn, Diet Chocolate Fudge cans, candy wrappers, and notebooks.

"Don't show this to my parents," groaned Elaine. "They'll never let me study at your place again." She started thumbing through the other photos, family pictures taken at the

61

beach. Zack! Elaine froze at the photo of Zack smiling at her.

"Hubba, hubba," said Alex. "Who's the hunk in the bathing suit?"

"That's no hunk." Karen laughed. "That's my brother."

Kit studied the photo. "He sure doesn't look like you," she said.

"Thanks, heaps," said Karen, comically squiggling her face.

"Oh, no." Kit blushed. "I didn't mean you weren't good-looking. I just meant..."

"I know," said Karen. "I'm the only one in my family with three eyes."

"No," said Kit laughing, "I meant the red hair."

"That, too," mugged Karen.

"Probably recessive genes," said Carl, standing. "If you all will excuse me, I have some work on the yearbook waiting for me."

"Go ahead," said Elaine. "I'll return our 'blanket.' It's the least I can do."

After he left, the girls quickly took the photos from Elaine, passing them around. Elaine listened miserably as all the girls oohed and ahhed over Zack. He was obviously the type girls fell for.

"Great body," said Alex. "He looks like an athlete."

"I'll bet he has a good sense of humor," said Lori. "Something in his eyes..."

"Definitely the playboy type," announced Kit. "I'd know that look anywhere."

"Wrong—all wrong," said Karen, shaking her head vigorously, making her halo of curls dance. "He's ugly and dumb, and the only exercise he gets is popping open beer cans and turning on the telly."

Elaine tried to laugh with the others, but she was upset by their comments. Zack probably *was* a playboy who had asked out tons of girls the same way he had asked her. Why hadn't she seen it before? If she broke up with Carl so she could date Zack, she'd end up with no one. Zack probably had girls lined up waiting for him. Poor Carl had only Elaine and, with the Apple audition coming up in two weeks, he needed her more than ever.

"I'll come with you," said Alex, helping Elaine fold and return the drop cloth and sheet. Later, as they walked to class, Alex asked, "Am I wrong, or do you seem a little more preoccupied than usual?"

Her beautiful almond-shaped eyes were filled with bold curiosity and concern. "No," confessed Elaine, "I...I have a few things on my mind."

"Like?"

She told Alex about her mom's pregnancy.

"There's something else bothering you," said Alex with her usual frankness. "We've been friends too long for you to cover up."

Elaine was silent a moment as they started to cut across the lawn to their class. "It's Carl . . ."

"He wants to break up?"

"No, no. It's nothing like that. I guess it's me, really. Well, actually, it's Zack."

"Karen's brother?" They slipped into the flow of students crisscrossing the quad. Elaine felt Alex waiting.

"Oh, Alex, I can't stop thinking about him!" Hot tears stung Elaine's eyes, and she wiped them away quickly.

Alex waited expectantly. "So?"

"So . . . I know it's wrong. I'm going with Carl."

Alex laughed. "Just because you're going with someone doesn't mean you can't still look. *Everyone* looks."

Elaine shook her head. "No. It's wrong. I have no right thinking about another boy. And I feel so bad about it, and so guilty."

"Elaine Gregory!" scolded Alex, "you are much too hard on yourself. If Zack Waverly is half as gorgeous in person as he is in his photos, how could a red-blooded American girl *not* think about him. Unless, of course"—she wiggled her dark eyebrows suggestively—"you've gone beyond the thinking stage."

"Alex!" Elaine's cheeks burned with embarrassment. "Isn't thinking about him bad enough?"

"Mrs. Kamala once said, 'All men have thoughts that would shame the devil.' I assume that goes for women, too." They followed the crowd entering the math building and moved to a quiet corner. "I can understand your obsession with Zack," sympathized Alex. "And romance is important, but you have to realize it's not everything."

Elaine looked at her friend in dismay. "I thought you'd tell me to 'go for it,'" she said, disappointed.

"I would have," agreed Alex, "if we'd talked *before* I broke up with Wes. Just because I can't bear watching him risk his life racing cars doesn't mean I don't still love him and think about him all the time."

"What does that have to do with me and Zack?"

"Elaine, sometimes you have to weigh what you're giving up with what you think you're getting." She put a comforting hand on Elaine's arm. "You'd be giving up Carl—who happens to be one of the nicest guys around—for Zack— who is a total unknown."

"But I can't stop thinking about him."

Alex squeezed her arm reassuringly. "Zack's new. He's exciting. But don't let that cloud everything you've shared with Carl." Alex reminded Elaine of the time Carl helped her organize a rally against the company that had unfairly fired Elaine's father—of how he rescued Elaine from being trampled by the crowd. The girls jumped as the class bell rang.

"Besides," said Alex, heading toward her class, "Zack may be gorgeous now, but just take a look at any one of your parents' high school reunion photos. High school 'hunks' have a way of growing bald and fat. I doubt Carl will ever have those problems." She called back over her shoulder, "Think about it."

Elaine couldn't focus on the trigonometry lecture. She stared at the solid band of black Z's she'd drawn on the border of her green notebook. She longed to write ZACKZACKZACK-ZACK but couldn't for fear Carl would borrow her notes. The Zs looked like an abstract design, and writing them made Elaine feel closer to Zack.

When she finished the border, she began a new row of Zs. This can't go on, she realized, slamming the pen down on the book. She was acting like a kid, like fourteen-year-old Andrea with one of her puppy-love crushes. Seventeen was too old for that kind of love. Alex was right. Elaine had to concentrate on Carl. She had to give their relationship the care and nurturing it deserved. She had to purge herself of Zack, get him out of her life. Totally. Completely. Forever.

He has to stop calling.

The thought came to her clearly, concisely, exactly. As long as she heard Zack's voice, she wouldn't be able to get him out of her system. She picked up her pen and continued her new row of Zs.

With tremendous sadness she realized there was no good way to tell a friend you didn't want to hear from him for a while. At the very least she owed Zack the courtesy of trying to explain her decision in person. The trick would be doing it without Zack suspecting the intensity of her feelings for him. But do it she must. Thoughts of Zack were messing up her life and jeopardizing the wonderful relationship she had with Carl.

Chapter Six

"This is fine," said Elaine as Alex eased the Green Demon up to the curb in front of the Student Union building.

"Sure you don't want me to wait?" asked Alex. "I wouldn't mind."

"I'm sure," Elaine said, grateful for her friend's support. This was something she had to do alone. "I'll grab a bus to the mall and walk home from there."

"Good luck," said Alex. "And don't look so gloomy. Making a clean break with Zack will be hard, but you're doing the right thing."

Elaine watched the Green Demon drive away and felt totally stranded on the unfamiliar Columbia Junior College campus. On impulse, she'd decided to see Zack immediately after school, to cut him out of her life cold turkey. She would just show up, say what she had to say, and go home. Not that she was at all sure *what* she was going to say.

Searching the map posted at the entrance to the sprawling campus, Elaine located the Speech Arts Building and began walking toward it. Zack said he'd be spending every afternoon before the festival in the editing room. It seemed to make more sense to face him at school than at his home, where Karen would be around to ask questions.

Feeling very young compared to the college students she passed, Elaine tried pretending she was a coed as she followed the brick path through the maze of buildings. Normally, she worked Monday, Tuesday, and Friday from four to eight. But the way she felt just now, she knew she'd go crazy if she had to wait until Wednesday to talk to Zack. At least this way, it would soon be over, and she could get on with her life. She wasn't much good to anyone in her present condition, especially not to a company that needed her to solder delicate stereo circuitry. She was grateful her supervisor at Orion Electronics had been understanding when she called to say she wouldn't be able to come to work. It was the first time she'd missed a day, and her supervisor rescheduled her for Wednesday.

Elaine stood outside the Speech Arts Building. Why did she feel sick to her stomach? Why was her heart pounding like a rock drum? "The journey of a thousand miles begins with but a single step." The phrase jumped into her thoughts, and she moved her foot forward up the first step. She wiped her damp hands on her shirt, taking a second step. Then the third . . .

A large sign inside the door said FILM DEPARTMENT—DOWNSTAIRS. Someone had written "Enter at your own risk" on the sign. Elaine started down, the sound of her sandals echoing softly on the deserted stairwell. She was nearly at the bottom when a loud bell startled her. All around her classroom doors banged open, a sea of laughing, talking, shouting students flooding the hall below.

Elaine felt drenched. Nervous perspiration, always her first response to tension, became worse. Hot, miserable, her courage failing, Elaine spun around to leave. Forgotten completely was the elaborate speech she'd outlined on her walk across campus.

"Elaine!" Zack's strong voice cut through the din of the students. He was immediately at her side, and she trembled as she felt his sinewy arm slip around her waist, guiding her effortlessly through the crowd and into the film lab.

"I can't believe it!" He laughed, turning her toward him, both hands on her waist.

It was impossible for her to breathe. He was there—holding her—his gunmetal blue eyes looking straight at her, into her, through her. It had been so long since she'd seen him in person. He was more overpowering than she remembered. How could she have forgotten the impact he had on her?

"Try and catch your breath," he said, tenderly brushing back a strand of her hair. "Students getting out of their last class of the day are a rough crowd to fight."

There was no way Zack could know she was out of breath from seeing him again. His lips were moving but it was a few moments before Elaine composed herself enough to focus on his words.

"...really can't believe you're here! What's the occasion?"

Elaine couldn't remember a single word of her speech.

"I...ummm...I'm here to...to do research." The gears in her mind whirred frantically, grasping for something to say.

"Research?"

"For my public speaking class. I need a Speech to Inform, and I'd like to do it on how films are made." She prayed her excuse didn't sound as lame to Zack as it did to her.

"Fabulous!" he said. "Come over here, I'll take you through step by step."

Elaine heaved a sigh of relief, following Zack around the film lab as he took her through the process.

"Sit!" he commanded, stationing her in front of a large console with three television monitors and several keyboards. "This has been my mistress for the past few weeks."

"She's lovely," said Elaine, cringing as her voice cracked.

"She's a pain," said Zack, bending over Elaine's chair, feeding a tape into the machine. Elaine swallowed nervously as he stood behind her guiding her hands over the video editing equipment. Elaine was powerfully aware of Zack and his nearness to her, barely noticing other students trickling into the room. For some reason her mind jumped to that night in her kitchen when she had brushed up against Carl, trying to interest him in a little romance. That was like walking through quicksand, she thought. Being close to Zack was like riding a comet. Be careful, she warned herself, or you'll get burned.

"Come on," Zack said suddenly, grabbing her hand and pulling her from the room, up the stairs, and out of the building.

"But where . . ."

"I've spent too many hours in that darned room. It's time to play some serious hooky."

They strolled slowly outside, savoring the fresh air. Zack held her hand casually, as if it were the most natural act in the world. How many other hands has he held like this, wondered Elaine. Zack would probably laugh if he

73

suspected the intense impact his touch was having on her. He gave her a guided tour of the campus, pointing out buildings and places of interest. Elaine smiled and nodded, not hearing a single word. Every atom of her being was focused on the feel of her hand in his.

"You look good on a campus," said Zack, leading her into the student union. As they were settling into a booth with their cups of coffee, a nearby group waved to Zack, calling him over. "Be right back," he said. He returned a minute later, laughing. "They wanted to know if you were a new transfer student," he said. "One guy was hoping you were my sister so I'd give him your number. That's the blessing *and* the curse of a small campus; everyone knows everyone else."

"They think I'm a college student?" asked Elaine, feeling suddenly older.

"Not too much longer before you join the ranks," said Zack. "Where do you think you'll go?"

"Well, I've been accepted to Stanford on a partial scholarship. I've been thinking of studying film."

"Good choice. That's where all the best demented minds wind up." Taking her hand in his, he kissed it. Elaine looked around, embarrassed. No one seemed to notice. "I am in your debt," he said, "for staying so close to Glendale. If you moved away, Karen would have no one to bug, except me."

"Thanks a lot." Elaine laughed, reluctantly forcing herself to ease her hand from his. Sitting there, surrounded by college students, made her feel wonderfully sophisticated. "Sometimes I can't wait to start college," she said, "and other times I'm scared stiff."

"Beginnings are like that," said Zack. "I still remember the terror I felt the first time I crossed the street all by myself. I think I was all of four years old. And the first time I took the car out by myself I was sweating so much my hands kept slipping on the wheel. Which was nothing compared to the nervousness of my first date. And my first . . ." He stopped suddenly, his face becoming a deep red.

Elaine stared at Zack, confused by his sudden shyness, so much like her own. She'd assumed someone who looked like Zack would be experienced in the romance department. It wouldn't have surprised her to hear him brag about his conquests, but she was amazed by his unexpected embarrassment.

"I'm surprised you remember your first date," she said.

"Are you kidding? I remember it like it was yesterday. As a matter of fact"—he raised his eyebrows rakishly—"it *was* yesterday."

"Very funny," said Elaine. "I'll bet anything you broke your first heart in preschool."

Zack shook his head solemnly. "My poor,

dear, misguided young lady, you are looking at a former ugly duckling, nerd, wimp, washout. A minus zero on the heart-throb scale."

"Oh, come on."

"Ask Karen, if you don't believe me. My little sister will be delighted to detail my former vast ugliness, right down to my large warts and green skin. Actually, I was two feet four inches until the end of my junior year in high school. It was hard on my social life, although I *did* get into the movies for half price."

"Zack Waverly . . ."

"It's the truth! I had an after-school job as a step stool in the Glendale library." He held up his right hand, his face the picture of total innocence. "Honest. This devastatingly handsome man you see before you is a relatively new development."

Elaine couldn't believe it. Zack? Handsome, brawny, "hunk," Zack?

"Well, Prince," said Elaine, "you might as well know you weren't the only frog in the pond." She told him about her recent metamorphosis. "Sometimes," she said, "I think the experience of being an unattractive child is like the grain of sand that turns an oyster into a pearl. If you can stand the pain, and wait it out, it can turn into something very beautiful."

"I must have needed a whole bucket of sand," said Zack. "I was a miniature wimp with a mouthful of railroad tracks and a reluctant thyroid gland. Then, practically overnight, I began to grow, and my voice deepened. Every morning I'd look into the mirror and feel like I'd invaded someone else's body. I swear, it was like entering *The Twilight Zone*."

"Doo-doo-doo-doo, doo-doo-doo." Elaine sang the show's theme song.

"Go ahead, make fun. But I felt like I'd hit a lush oasis after sixteen years on the desert. I started going out with anyone and everyone in sight."

"It sounds like you were busy," said Elaine.

"*Frantic* is more like it. It wasn't until I realized I didn't totally gross out women that I calmed down enough to become more selective. Now," he said, "for the first time in my life, I have the luxury of deciding the type of girl I really want to be with. But I don't ever think I'll forget what it feels like to be ignored by the opposite sex."

"Don't I know it," Elaine sympathized. "No one ever seemed able to see beyond my I.Q. 'Elaine the Brain' they called me. If a boy *did* talk to me, it was to ask about the algebra assignment. Not really great for the ego."

"That explains so much about you," he said softly, his eyes searching hers.

"Me, too, about you," said Elaine, meeting his eyes for a full heartbeat before looking down at her coffee. *This is all wrong,* she thought. *I'm supposed to be steering away from Zack, not*

heading right for him. Yet, she felt herself opening in a new way, sensing a part of herself reaching out to this fabulously unique person who
was becoming a part of her life. She fought to
push the feelings aside.

"Of course," she said, "it was partly my fault.
I never did anything to make myself more attractive, and I know I sometimes used my intel-
lect as a shield. It was like I was daring people to
like me. There was something so scary about
letting someone get close to me."

"Like Carl?" Zack's eyes held hers, and
Elaine sensed the deeper meaning in his
question.

"Yes," she said softly. "It took a rugged indi-
vidual to barge through my defenses. Carl was
there when I needed someone, and I'm grateful
to him for so many things."

"Grateful?" A slight smile played on Zack's
lips. "I'm *grateful* to my English lit professor for
an A. But I'd hardly want to have a romance
with him. Is there anything between you and
Carl beyond gratitude?"

Elaine wiped a drop of perspiration from her
forehead. "It's very warm in here," she said. "I
. . . I think I should be getting back." She slid
from the booth, hurrying out. Zack followed
close behind her.

"Let me drive you home," he said, catching up
to her.

"You have work to do," said Elaine, not daring

to turn toward him.

"Let me drive you home," he said again, gently gripping her arm. "Please."

Elaine allowed him to lead her to his car. Neither of them talked on the way home. Zack pulled up to the curb a few houses before Elaine's.

"Elaine," he said, "I'm not going to apologize to you."

She stared straight ahead, torn between wanting to flee from the car and wanting to stay. She gasped softly as the butterfly touch of his fingertips caressed her chin and turned her head toward him.

"I'm not sure what's happening," he said, his voice husky with emotion, "but I know I'm feeling something for you I've never felt before. I'm supposed to be editing my film, and half the time I wind up staring into the monitor and seeing your face."

"Zack. Don't. I . . . Carl and I . . ."

Zack sank back into his seat, staring out the front window, his knuckles turning white as he gripped the steering wheel. "Don't you think I keep telling myself you have a boyfriend? That you're taken? Don't you think I know I have no right to make demands on you?"

The force of emotion in his voice pulled Elaine toward him. She struggled to fight the rising tide of feelings in herself. He turned toward her, and she saw the struggle reflected in his face.

"What confuses me," he said, stroking her cheek with his thumb, "is how I can feel so strongly about you and not have you feel anything for me." His eyes pleaded for a promise she could not give.

"Zack, I . . . I'm very fond . . ."

"Which is why I have to know what else you feel for Carl besides gratitude."

Elaine could barely breathe, let alone think. She felt as if high voltage were crackling crazily through her body. The skin on her face burned under his touch. "There's friendship," she said shakily, struggling to find the right words. "And caring. Deep, deep caring."

Zack caressed her face in his hands, bringing her face to his.

"What about love?" he asked softly, kissing her left cheek. "And romance?" He kissed her right cheek. "And desire?" His warm lips moved gently onto hers. Elaine closed her eyes—falling, falling, falling into a world that was only she and Zack.

Her heart beat so hard she could hardly breathe. Zack's kiss was everything she had ever dreamed a kiss could be. Should be. His arms encircled her, pulling her close . . . so close.

"*Is, too!*" Chrissie's shrill voice pierced Elaine's dreamworld. The twins stood on the front porch of the house, fighting.

"*Is not,*" screamed Carla. "That's not Carl."

"Is *too* Elaine," insisted Chrissie.

"Oh, no, the twins," moaned Elaine, snapping back to reality. "I've got to go."

Flustered, confused, unable to look at Zack, she hurriedly gathered her books and fumbled for the doorknob.

"Elaine, you can't leave me like this. I've got to know...."

"Don't you see," said Elaine, her eyes begging for understanding. "This is exactly how I have to leave you. I have no choice."

"Of course you have a choice. Elaine..."

She ran from the car to the house, up the stairs, and into the safety inside.

Chapter Seven

Elaine rushed up to her room, her long legs taking the narrow attic stairs two at a time. Throwing herself onto her bed, she gripped her pillow tightly, sobbing into it, trying to stop shaking.

I've betrayed Carl, she thought guiltily, betrayed our trust in each other. What had happened? What had gone wrong? Her visit to Zack, which was supposed to break off their relationship, may have instead sparked the beginnings of a full-fledged romance. Why hadn't she left things as they were? Now, there was no going back. No longer could she pretend to herself or Zack that theirs was a platonic friendship.

Meow, meow. Munchkin jumped onto the

bed, curling into a ball next to Elaine.

"Your timing's lousy," she said, stroking his silky coat. Carl had known Munchkin was just what she'd needed when her own precious cat had been killed by a truck. Kind Carl. Thoughtful Carl.

"Rrrrrrrrr." Munchkin rumbled contentedly.

"Sorry," said Elaine, picking Munchkin up and carrying him to the door, "I don't need any reminders of Carl just now."

Meow? Munchkin blinked his beautiful Siamese eyes at her.

"Don't worry." Elaine smiled, nuzzling his fur with her nose. "Whatever else happens, you always have a home with me." She set him in the hall and closed the door.

Elaine found her junior yearbook in the bookcase near the door. Taking it down, she rested it on her dresser, leafing through it to the large photo of Zack in his varsity soccer uniform. He stood defiantly, strong arms folded, muscled legs set apart, head tilted cockily at the camera, a devilish grin on his face as if he were about to tackle the photographer. For the first time in her life, Elaine felt the pain of wanting someone she should not be wanting. If only Zack had ignored her! But he wanted her. He wanted her with an intensity that frightened her.

"So," she said, looking up into her dresser mirror, "just what are you going to do? You've gone from no boyfriends to two. They're both

84

great. They're both special."

She put baby oil on a tissue and wiped the tear-streaked black mascara from her cheeks. "But if you break up with Carl now, before his Apple interview, just when he needs you to be there supporting him, rooting for him, you're not the woman I think you are." She pulled her dark hair, so hot on her neck, into a ponytail. "On the other hand, Zack is miserable. And it's all your fault for going to see him today. So, what are you going to do?" Her puffy red eyes stared back mutely. "Thanks a lot. You're a great help."

"Elaine?"

Elaine jumped at the sound of her mother's voice calling nearby.

"Yes?"

"Oh, good, I thought I heard you in your room. I'm over in the cedar closet. Can you give me a hand?"

"Be right there." Elaine splashed cold water on her face from the old "servants' sink" in her room. It helped a little, but her eyes were still swollen. She headed out of her room, across the cavernous attic crammed with furniture waiting for the magic touch of her mother's refinishing tools. She found her mother in the large closet her parents had built to store out-of-season clothing.

Elaine breathed in the delicious smell of the cedar wood, which her father said was supposed to discourage moths. Her mother sat in the middle of the floor, surrounded by piles of clothing Elaine recognized from the twins. Mrs. Gregory looked so tranquil amidst the chaos that Elaine couldn't help laughing.

"I thought you sold all this stuff at the garage sale," said Elaine.

"How could I part with these?" asked her mother, lovingly holding up a tiny hand-knit sweater with matching bonnet and booties. "Aren't they the most precious things you ever saw?"

She set them on her small mound of a stomach, as if to see if the set would fit the new baby.

Elaine laughed. "Perfect."

Her mother looked around wearily at the piles of unsorted garments. "I honestly always meant to put these things away according to size," she explained, "but I never seemed to find the time. Could you help me sort through them?"

"Sure," said Elaine, clearing a place on the floor for herself. She began going through the pile, trying to find the tiny size label in each garment. She felt her mother working busily alongside her. For a long time, they worked in easy silence.

"There's something soothing about doing a mindless activity," said her mother. "Not many of my friends understand why I like ironing. But I find it gives me time to relax my brain."

"That's one of the reasons I like my job at Orion," said Elaine. "I never really thought about it before, but I guess my soldering is like your ironing. It's become automatic, and my time at work's one of the few times of the week my mind can be still. In fact, sometimes I wonder if I should be looking for a more challenging job."

"There will be time enough for mind-bending jobs when you finish school and go out into the 'real world.'" She glanced at her watch. "Aren't you home early?"

"Oh, I...I had some things to do after school, so I'm going to Orion tomorrow, instead."

Her mother smiled admiringly. "I swear I don't know how you juggle all your activities and responsibilities."

Elaine looked down, quickly pulling small garments from the nearest pile. She'd started sweating, as much from nervousness as from the heat of the cedar closet. She was grateful her mother hadn't asked what those "things to do after school" were. Elaine couldn't have told her mom about Zack. Not yet. Not when her own thoughts and feelings were so mixed up. She threw herself into the job, relieved to have something to do.

Slowly the mess of clothing began to take shape, surrounding Elaine and her mother with stacks of tiny size-coordinated outfits. Elaine had become so engrossed in her work that she wasn't sure when her mother had stopped, but a sixth sense told her her mother was regarding her closely. Elaine looked up into her mother's concerned blue eyes.

"It's the baby, isn't it?" asked Mrs. Gregory tenderly.

"The baby?" asked Elaine, confused.

"Hon, I can tell how terribly upset you are right now." She rested her hand on her growing stomach. "And, even though you tried to hide it, I knew from the beginning you resented this pregnancy."

"Oh, Mom, I'm sorry," said Elaine. "It was just a reflex reaction. I promise. You caught me off guard. I'll get used to the idea. Truly I will."

"I understand how you feel," comforted Mrs. Gregory. "Remember, I was your age when my father died. Grandma had to go to work, which meant I cared for four younger brothers and sisters after school. There were times I felt resentment. More times than I care to remember."

"I don't mean to seem selfish," said Elaine.

"Selfish?" Her mother gently squeezed Elaine's hand. "You are perfectly normal. You show me an oldest child who doesn't resent her siblings every now and then, and I'll show you a household with a live-in baby-sitter."

Elaine laughed, reaching over to hug her mother. She breathed in her mother's soothing smells of lavender, wildflowers, spices. Mrs. Gregory used natural beauty products from the health food store, which smelled more beautiful to Elaine than all the hundred-dollar perfumes at Macy's perfume counter.

"And I promise," said Mrs. Gregory, lovingly brushing back a strand of Elaine's hair, "I'll try not to lean on your wonderfully strong shoulders too much."

Elaine noticed how much healthier her mother looked now than she had just a few months before. Once plump, Mrs. Gregory had become gaunt during the time her husband was out of work. With the pregnancy, her face had filled out and taken on a rosy glow.

"Mom, can I ask you a very personal question?"

"You can ask me anything," said Mrs. Gregory. "If it's too personal to answer, I'll let you know."

"Was this baby an accident, or did you and Daddy plan it? I mean, after the hard times we've just gone through, weren't you afraid of taking on another responsibility?"

"This baby was planned, Elaine. This may be hard for you to understand just now, but there is a richness a child brings into the world with it. A joyousness. Daddy and I never talk about it, but we went through another hard time when you and Andrea were little. And I'll tell you, the outside world could do whatever it wanted to do to me, and I'd come home and see my beautiful children, and I'd be able to face anything."

"I...I didn't know," said Elaine. "For some reason I always thought you and Dad lived the good life."

"Oh, the worst of it was over so long ago," said her mother, "there never seemed any point in talking about it. But one thing's for sure, Elaine. When you've gone through the bad times, it makes you appreciate the good all that much more. You want to grab the happiness you can while you can."

Zack's face flashed in Elaine's mind, and she forced it quickly aside.

"It's been eight years since we've had a baby around this old house," said Mrs. Gregory. "You'll be going off to college soon and, while no one can ever take your special place, maybe it will be a little less lonely around here with a baby. With Andrea and the twins in school, the days have a way of getting pretty long for me."

"I hadn't thought of that," admitted Elaine. "I was thinking of all the work a new baby would mean—for all of us. I forgot about the happiness a baby brings."

"Don't try and force your emotions," cautioned Mrs. Gregory. "I don't expect you to love this baby just now. I remember I wanted to feel love from the moment I learned I was pregnant with you. I was too embarrassed to admit to anyone that I didn't. Then you were born, and the doctor put you into my arms, and at that instant I was overwhelmed with a love I could never have imagined. So don't worry about this baby. Everything will work out all right. I promise. Now, we'd better try and make a dent in this mess."

They attacked the piles with renewed vigor.

Mrs. Gregory was the only woman Elaine knew who was happiest around the home. Having a mother who was "just a housewife" used to embarrass Elaine, whose friends' mothers were all doing such exciting things in the "real" world. Lori's mother was an attorney for the Civil Liberties Union. Alex's mother had her own graphics design business. Kit's mom worked for a large corporation. Karen's mother was a veterinarian.

Elaine glanced up at her mother. Rita Gregory had had to work from the day she graduated from high school. She'd promised herself that, when she married and had children, she would stay home and make her family her work. For the first time Elaine realized her mother was a rare woman who was lucky enough to know exactly what made her happy. Even when it was out of fashion.

Elaine wished she felt happier about the baby, but she couldn't. Luckily, her mother understood. And, quite honestly, the baby was the least of Elaine's worries. Oh, why couldn't she be more like her mother? Why couldn't she decide exactly what she wanted, and then go after it? Her mother had a will of iron. Elaine's was more like soggy pudding. Especially after that scene in Zack's car. *My motto*, mused Elaine glumly, *should be "On your mark, get set, wait a minute."* She almost longed for the good old days when she had no boyfriends. It may have been lonely, but it sure was a lot less complicated.

"Don't try to force your emotions," her mother had said. And maybe Elaine was trying to force feelings for Carl that weren't there. She wished she could ask her mother what she should do about the other kind of emotion. The kind a Zack Waverly created. Emotion that stampeded crazily, wildly, dragging you helplessly in its wake.

Wednesday, 1:00 a.m.—Up nearly 20 hours—
Can't sleep.

ZACK KISSED ME!!!!!!!!!!!!!!!!

Hard. On the lips. I've never EVER been kissed
like that! Nobody has! Not in the entire history
of the world!!!

ZACKKISSEDMEZACKKISSEDMEZACK
KISSEDMEZACKKISSEDME

How can I describe it? (Since it won't happen
again, I'd like to try to capture the moment for
my great-grandchildren, who will surely want
to read all the journals I intend to keep . . . espe-
cially the juicy parts. Not that my great-grand-

mothers ever did anything juicy.)

The kiss was sort of a cross between Carl's kiss (Carl is my boyfriend. Yes, I am going with someone. Which is precisely why I will not be kissing Zack Waverly again, not that I kissed him), and the kisses I see on the "soaps."

Carl's kisses (as far as I can remember) are exactly like he is: gentle and sweet and, well, nice.

As for kisses on the soaps, Mom says they remind her of people eating watermelon. All openmouthed and sloppy. To tell the truth, I was a little afraid Zack might kiss that way (I hadn't planned this kiss, but I did dream about it...just a little...like all the time. It won't, of course, happen again).

But Zack's kiss was none of the above. It was PERFECT. My fingertips are still tingling, and I swear I can feel my heart beating when I think about IT. Of course, I am in a weakened condition. I've been awake almost one full day, and my mind may not be working very well. Tomorrow Zack's kiss may seem like nothing at all. (Which is just as well, since it mustn't happen ever again.)

I am writing this in the kitchen. I'm drinking hot mint tea and munching frozen chocolate chips from a bag I keep in the freezer for "this time of the month." I'm not much of a chocolate eater except when I get this craving. Then, look out. This is an emotionally un-

94

stable time of month for me, which probably explains why I am making such a Big Deal out of ZACK'S KISS.

ZACK WAVERLY KISSED ME!!!!

There. I've said it. I feel better for having written it out. Now it's over and done. Finished.

I am glad I experienced at least one such kiss in my life. Most women never will. At least I will have the memory of that magic moment (since I can't let it happen again) to carry with me through the years.
Your friend,

Elaine the Vamp

Chapter Eight

The days following THE KISS were a nightmare. Elaine lived in a constant fog, walking past her friends on the quad, forgetting her books in her locker, leaving her lunch on the counter at home, turning out half the usual number of circuit boards on her job.

"How did your meeting with Zack go?" Alex had asked on Wednesday.

"Zack? Meeting?"

Alex frowned at Elaine, puzzled. "I could have sworn you were the tall, thin brunette I dropped off at Columbia College yesterday after school."

"Oh, *that* meeting," Elaine said vaguely. "Zack showed me around campus. It's nice." She wandered off.

"Uh, Elaine?" Lori had come up behind

Elaine on Thursday, stopping her on the quad.

"Yes?" Elaine noticed Lori had pulled her blond hair up and over to one side, creating a combination innocent/sophisticated look. She studied Lori's hairstyle, trying to figure out how it was done so she could copy it.

"I don't mean to pry . . ."

"Yes?"

"But are you undergoing some sort of initiation for a club?"

"Nooooo," said Elaine, looking puzzled.

"Well, are you paying off on a bet you lost?"

Elaine shook her head. "No. Why?"

Lori looked down at Elaine's feet. "Then why are you wearing two different colored socks, neither of which comes close to matching a single thing you have on?"

Elaine looked down, startled by the bright yellow and bright orange socks. "Oh," she said, smiling weakly. "Well, would you believe I have a pair just like this at home?"

That afternoon, Alex and Lori had forced Elaine to go with them to Gennaro's to visit Kit at work.

"Nothing like a piece of mediocre pizza to get a person back to normal," said Alex, leading the way to the front counter.

"Of course, this isn't as good as mediocre," said Lori, "but it will have to do."

"The usual?" asked Kit, pencil poised to take their order. She rolled her eyes sideways, signaling she was unable to talk because Mr. Watkins was lurking near the kitchen doorway.

"Noooo," said Alex, loudly enough for the surly owner to hear. "I think we'll settle for only one large pizza today."

"And a giant salad," said Lori.

"Coming right up," Kit said, passing the order through the kitchen portal to Justin. "Go sit down," whispered Kit. "I'll bring the order when it's ready."

Alex had scanned the booths, leading them to the one with the fewest rips and tears in the faded red leatherette. Elaine couldn't seem to pay attention to the conversation Alex and Lori were having about stick shift versus automatic transmissions. Instead, she stared at the dust patterns on the plastic plants. It was the silence that finally made her look up. Both friends were staring at her.

"You have the strangest look on your face," said Lori.

"Sort of a half smile," said Alex.

"You know I haven't smiled with my teeth since I wore braces," explained Elaine.

"Elaine, no kid with braces ever had that particular look on her face," said Alex. "It was strictly X-rated."

Later, Elaine, who hated anchovies, somehow ate two slices of Alex's half of the pizza, which Justin had heaped with extra anchovies. She was up half that night drinking water.

By Friday, her friends had given up all hope of communicating with Elaine.

"Earth to Elaine. Earth to Elaine. Come in. Over." Carl's voice broke into her thoughts. Elaine realized she'd been standing in front of her locker, staring. "It helps to open the locker if you want to see what's inside."

Elaine looked at Carl, dazed. She'd been reliving Zack's kiss, the feel of his hands on her face, his arms around her ...

"Hello in there?" Carl again.

Elaine forced herself back to reality. She'd gone over the edge. Until THE KISS she had been able to function as a normal human being. Well, relatively normal. Not now. Not anymore.

"Oh, hi, Carl," she said, studying his face intently, hoping to feel even the slightest little spark.

Twinkling hazel eyes flecked with orange.

Nothing.

Shaggy brown hair with a will of its own.

More nothing.

High cheekbones and soft, full lips.

Nothing, nothing, nothing.

She sighed deeply, turning back to her locker.

This isn't fair to Carl, she thought unhappily, but she couldn't seem to help herself. She yanked open her locker, rummaging through it angrily. Maybe if Carl told her he loved her once in a while, maybe if he grabbed her and kissed her ... Maybe this wasn't all her fault. Maybe he was partly to blame. But, even as she thought it, she knew it wasn't true. Carl was the same wonderful Carl he'd always been. She couldn't blame him for changes she was going through, even though blaming him would make her feel a lot less guilty.

"Uh, um, Carl. About this weekend," began Elaine, unable to look Carl in the eye. How she dreaded telling him about her plans for Saturday night. Up to that moment, she'd hoped Carl might come up with something wonderful to do. Something exciting and creative and irresistible. Something that would rekindle the old fire she used to feel when she saw him, talked to him, *thought* about him.

"Glad you mentioned it," he said brightly. "I'm borrowing my cousin's newspaper computer program Saturday night." He talked excitedly as they headed across the quad to physics. "It has different type fonts. Old English, italics, boldface. It's a great program. I can only have it until Sunday, and I want to make stationery for my family. Figure out what you want — business cards, stationery, invitations, whatever — and I'll print it."

Elaine tried to look interested as Carl pulled samples of the computer program's type from his backpack. It was useless to hope Carl would ever sweep her off her feet. As he talked, she began imagining the breakup scene she knew was imminent. If only she could create an ending that wouldn't be painful.

"Sounds like fun," she said, as they entered the classroom and took their seats. She swallowed nervously at the half truth she was about to tell. "But I promised Karen I'd go with her and her family to the Columbia Film Festival." No need to mention Zack.

"Hey, great. Now I don't feel so guilty about not being with you." The idea of not being with Elaine didn't seem to bother him at all. Elaine wondered if he cared anything for her anymore.

Later, when Mr. Byer asked for a volunteer to demonstrate the principles of inertia, Carl went up to the front of the room. "We will now see how matter at rest tends to remain at rest," said Mr. Byer, whipping a sheet off a large board studded with nails.

Elaine watched impassively as Carl eased his body onto the bed of nails. She didn't flinch when Mr. Byer placed a square concrete block on Carl's chest. She felt only intellectual curiosity when Mr. Byer whacked the block with a sledgehammer, breaking it in two.

Elaine knew the nails were closely spaced to distribute Carl's weight evenly over them. She knew the concrete block's inertia stopped the sledgehammer from forcing his body downward. Physics was so simple, she thought. So clear. So exact. If only love were that clear-cut.

As she watched the other students go up to check Carl's back for signs of nail wounds, it occurred to her that Mr. Byer couldn't have selected a more appropriate student for his demonstration. When it came to romance, *Inertia* was Carl Schmidt's middle name.

Elaine began making a border of *Z*s on her physics notebook, thinking out her breakup scene with Carl, trying once again to give it a happy ending.

Friday, 9:00 p.m.
In bed, going to sleep early for a change.

Dear Journal,
    5 minutes have gone by since I wrote "Dear Journal."
    10 minutes
    15 minutes
    20 minutes
    25 minutes
    One half of an entire hour.
    That does it. I can't think of anything to write. So good night.
    Oh, I aced that French quiz I took Tuesday. Well, I guess that's about all.
    Except, some nerd pulled the fire alarm to-

day while I was in gym. Why couldn't he/she have done it during physics when I'm dying for fresh air? I was already outside and had finally gotten a chance to be goalie in soccer. Ain't my day. (Is a female nerd a nerdette?)

Okay. okay. So you're wondering about Zack. I overreacted. It was just a kiss. Zack's just a friend. A gorgeous, knockout, witty, sexy friend. But a friend, nonetheless. Got that? Good.

Not feeling too happy. Am rethinking my relationship with Carl. Not ready to talk about it just now. Sorry.

'Nite.

Elaine

Chapter Nine

"Elaine!" Andrea's voice echoed up the attic staircase. "The Waverlys are here."

"Be right there," shouted Elaine, unhappily buttoning up the thirteenth outfit she'd tried on. No time to change again. It would have to do. She tucked the aqua blouse into the mid-calf black skirt. The yellow suspenders, which had seemed such fun when she'd put them on, looked ridiculously loud and childish. Pulling them off, she tossed them onto the pile of rejected outfits on her bed and raced downstairs.

"Welcome aboard," said Karen, springing out of the car to hold the door open for Elaine. Elaine stared in disbelief at the bits of glitter sparkling in Karen's tangle of red curls. Karen's beautiful eyes were obscured by comical oversized sunglasses. There were so many petticoats under her full-skirted fifties dress, it popped up in front when she slid in next to Elaine.

Karen's boyfriend, Jeff Becker, sat on the other side of Elaine. He'd tried taming his shaggy blond hair with a gel, but it looked as though the curl in his hair had gotten the upper hand. She noticed he'd changed from his usual jeans and torn T-shirt into cords and a conservative beige button-down shirt.

"Well, *you* look nice, Jeff," Elaine said. "I'm not so sure about what's-her-name here."

"This is the Oscars, dahhhhling," Karen gushed. "One must dress ever so carefully, don't you know?"

"Mrs. Waverly," groaned Elaine, "how could you let her out of the house *dressed* that way?"

"That's what I asked," said Jeff, wrinkling his nose in disgust.

"Dressed what way?" asked Mrs. Waverly. "Do you notice anything unusual about your sister?" she asked Fred.

"Nooooo," said Karen's lanky oldest brother in his thoughtful, serious way, "can't say as I do. Actually, I thought Karen looked a bit underdressed tonight."

"Don't mind them," said Karen. "They've joined a support group founded by Madonna's family."

Elaine shook her head. "I can't believe I was

worried my pale mauve eye shadow was too daring. What's Zack going to say when he sees you?"

"Nothing. He'll probably just kill me. Quickly. Painlessly." Karen looked out over the tops of the glasses. "Actually, I'm good for him. He's much too serious. I wish he'd find something in his life besides that darn editing machine."

He has, thought Elaine. *He's found me.*

"I'm much more interesting than some people," intoned Karen, peering at Jeff, "who become positively boring when they 'dress up.' Beige is for bankers and brokers."

Karen and Jeff, who always reminded Elaine of sparring partners more than boyfriend and girl friend, began trading high-spirited insults. Elaine half listened, barely able to contain her excitement at the prospect of seeing Zack. Now that she'd made the decision to break up with Carl, she felt she was leaving one part of her life and moving on to the next. In a way, she felt as if she were about to leap from one rooftop to another. The scary part, of course, was the dark, foreboding abyss between them. Elaine knew a lot of girls who didn't break up with their old boyfriends until they'd lined up replacements. She couldn't do that to Carl. She'd decided not to say anything to Zack, not to make a commitment, until her relationship with Carl was over.

Jeff began talking baseball with Fred, and

Elaine leaned over, whispering to Karen.

"What happened to Silvano Bussetti?" she asked.

"Who?" Karen asked innocently.

"You remember, the gorgeous Italian you were going to invite who loved the way you compared him to Woody Allen."

"My luck." Karen pouted. "He found a girl who told him he looked like David Bowie. Let's face it," she said, "life is like the Oscars. We comedians get a lot of lip service, but we never win the prize." Elaine was happy Karen didn't seem upset. Jeff was the perfect boyfriend for her, and it bothered Elaine that Karen seemed to need to have future boyfriends ready and waiting in the wings. She looked at her funny, frizzy-haired friend. Sometimes it was hard to know what Karen was up to. She was brilliant at hiding her feelings behind a wall of wisecracks and one liners.

The auditorium was mobbed, a chaos of students, parents, and friends.

"Do you see Zack?" asked Mrs. Waverly. They searched the crowd but couldn't find him. "Never mind," she said, "I see some friends over there. Do you kids want to sit with me?"

"You never sit close enough," said Karen. "We're going up front." Fred stayed with Mrs. Waverly. Karen marched Elaine and Jeff to the second row, directly behind a group of male students.

"Sorry, excuse me, ooops." Elaine blushed furiously as Karen, bracelets clanging, skirts rustling, large purse banging, made her way into the seats. A few of the boys turned to stare, not bothering to conceal their surprise at Karen's outfit.

"This *is* where I catch the eight fifteen bus to Pomona, isn't it?" she asked perfectly seriously.

"No," said the boy in front of her, "that stops at row three."

"I never saw her before in my life," Elaine said to Jeff, leaning away from Karen.

"Saw who?" asked Jeff, looking around. They rolled their eyes as Karen dragged popcorn from her oversized bag and passed it around to everyone near them. In moments, she had put total strangers completely at ease.

How does she do it, Elaine wondered admiringly. In a million years, Elaine couldn't go up to strangers like that—unless, of course, she was hiding inside her Wilbur the Wildcat costume at a football game. Maybe Karen's outfit was her costume. Elaine checked her purse again for the box of Junior Mints she'd gift wrapped for Zack. He'd once told her it was physically impossible to watch a movie without a box of Junior Mints. Elaine was disappointed she wouldn't see him before the movies, but she decided to give it to him after the festival like an award. Picturing the surprise and delight on his face made her smile . . . straight into the face of the boy turned around in the seat in front of her.

"Hi, yourself," he said, raising an eyebrow suggestively.

The lights dimmed. "Saved by the film," Elaine whispered to herself with relief.

Ten films were listed on the program, each of them five minutes long.

By the end of the fifth film, Karen was sliding down into her seat, her stiff petticoats forming a shield between her and the screen. "I'm not going to make it," she gasped, clutching her chest. Elaine had to agree. She found the films amateurish, done by students more interested in innovative camera angles than story line.

"Hitchcock hated 'creative' camera angles," whispered Elaine as they waited for the next film to begin. "He couldn't figure out why so many young directors shot scenes with fields of flowers in the foreground, when flowers had nothing to do with the film."

"I wish he'd taught this group," said Karen. "If Zack uses a flower, I'm locking him out of the house. Forever."

The next four films weren't much better. Some were less offensive than others, but none stood out. Zack's film was listed last on the program.

"The teacher decided to show the films alphabetically according to the students' first names," Karen explained as they waited for Zack's film to begin.

"That's weird," said Jeff.

"I think there was a method to his madness," said Karen. "Or is it a madness to his method? Anyway, it's obvious he wanted Zack to be last. I figure either Zack's film's so bad everyone will be numb by the time it's screened, or it's so good the teacher hopes the audience will forget the nine that came before it."

The lights dimmed. There were no credits on the screen. Instead, the film began with the screen black, lightening slowly as a child's voice said, "My daddy's on a diet."

"Oh?" said Zack's voice. "And what does it mean to be on a diet?"

The picture took shape. A man and woman sat next to each other, watching Zack interview their child.

"A diet means Daddy gets to eat the cookies I bring home from school...and we don't tell Mommy."

The audience roared at the expressions on the parents' faces. Elaine's heart soared. It was obvious Zack's film was better than good! Zack had brought a group of preschoolers and their parents into a room and separated them into two groups. He had a camera on the children and one on the parents. As he questioned the children about everything from politics to love, he cut between their answers and their parents' faces. Elaine thrilled to the sounds of the festival audience howling as the parents reacted to their children's hilarious answers with surprise, anger, embarrassment, delight, agony, the whole range of human emotions.

Zack's film was fresh, innovative, funny. Best of all, it looked so simple and effortless that only film students or film buffs like Elaine would realize the incredible amount of work that had gone into it. The editing was subtle, camera work smooth, lighting and sound well thought out.

"They loved it!" shrieked Karen as the crowd applauded and whistled enthusiastically. All around them Elaine heard people say Zack's film was sure to win first prize.

"Your brother's great," said one of the boys in front of them.

"You're just saying that because I'm feeding you popcorn," said Karen. She sounded casual, but Elaine could tell how excited her friend was by how tightly she squeezed her hand and Jeff's as the awards were presented.

"And, our first prize," said the film professor, "is awarded to Zack Waverly."

"Way to go, Zack!" yelled Karen, jumping up and cheering. The entire audience laughed at her unbridled enthusiasm. A part of Elaine longed to cheer like Karen, to express her emotions openly and immediately, but Elaine sank embarrassed into her chair, trying to disappear from the staring crowd.

"Let's find him," said Karen as the house

lights came up. Jeff stayed behind as the girls rushed up to the crowded stage. As she made her way into the wings, Elaine's feet got tangled in a jumbled mass of curtain ropes. She could see Zack backstage and waved to him, but he didn't see her in the crush of filmmakers and well-wishers.

"Come on," said Karen impatiently.

"I'll be right there," said Elaine, laughing as she tugged at the ropes. "I seem to be tied up at the moment."

"Everyone's a comedian." Karen sighed, bending down to help. "I swear I don't know how you managed before you met me."

Finally free, Elaine started toward Zack. She froze as a coed in tight jeans, low-buttoned blouse, and waist-length blond hair rushed up to him. The girl flung herself at Zack, jumping up and down, hugging and kissing him. Elaine stood staring, feeling as if she'd been punched in the stomach.

"What now?" asked Karen, trying to pull Elaine toward Zack. "What's the matter?" Seeing the shock on Elaine's face, she followed Elaine's eyes to where Zack was embracing the girl. "Oh, no," said Karen sympathetically, "don't tell me you've gone and fallen for Old What's-His-Name?" She put a comforting arm around Elaine, and they watched as the blond girl pressed herself against Zack.

"If she gets any closer, he'll be wearing her,"

said Karen. "Let's get out of here."

Karen led Elaine away, joining the flow of the crowd out of the auditorium.

"It never occurred to me to tell you about Zack's girl friend," Karen apologized. "I just wouldn't have guessed you had a thing for Zack. You never said anything."

"I . . . I couldn't," said Elaine miserably.

"Of course, I knew you two liked each other from the way our phone bill doubled since Zack met you. And, the first time I saw you two together I thought I felt a little magic happening between you. But you never pumped me for information about Zack, or anything, and every time I heard him on the phone with you, he was talking about the movies. Since you were going with Carl, I figured you and Zack were just friends." She shook her head. "You and Zack. And I always thought you had good taste in men." She tried to get a smile from Elaine. Elaine shrugged, pretending not to be hurt.

"I'll be all right," she said. "It just caught me by surprise. I . . . I didn't know he was going with anyone. There's nothing between us. I mean, maybe there nearly was, but we're just friends." She babbled on and on, not giving Karen a chance to ask any questions.

In the car on the way home, Elaine thought how happy she should be that things hadn't gotten any farther than they had. At least she'd learned the truth about Zack before she'd ruined her relationship with Carl. What a disaster that would have been.

Later, lying on her bed, staring up at the stars through the skylight, she felt empty inside. Hollow. Numb. She didn't move when she heard the faint ring of the hall phone. Even when Andrea called her to the phone she moved slowly, as though she were in a dream.

"Well?" Zack's voice was buoyant, expectant. "What did you think?"

I think you're a flirt, a heartbreaker, a tease, a toyer with emotions, a playboy.... I think you've hurt me beyond hurt and I'll never trust my heart again. Not ever. That's what I think.

"I...I'm busy now." Her voice was flat and lifeless. "I can't talk. Bye." She hung up, turning to the wide-eyed Andrea. "No more calls for me tonight," she said.

"Oh, boy," said Andrea, "can I take yours?"

"All of them," said Elaine, trudging back up the stairs to her room.

"Even the boys?"

"*Especially* the boys."

Saturday night.

Dear Journal,
  When I was seven years old, Mom and Dad bought me a goldfish. It was my first pet. I loved that goldfish. I fed it every day, moved it around my bedroom so it wouldn't get bored with the same view, changed its water. I talked to it, read to it, cared for it. It was the first living thing (besides my family) I can remember really loving.
  Because the fish bowl was so small, I'd fill the water nearly to the top so my fish would have more room to swim. One day I came home from school and, as always, I ran upstairs to say hello to my fish. It was lying on

my floor. Dead. It had jumped out of its bowl.

I hadn't thought about that moment for years. Not until tonight. Tonight, I relived that horrible, helpless, agonizing pain of losing something I'd loved.

Zack Waverly has a girl friend.

E.

120

Chapter Ten

"Remember last month when my mom made me and my stepdad spend that dumb 'get to know each other better' day together?" Carl asked.

"Uh-huh," said Elaine, trying to pay attention as they locked their bikes to the rack outside Glenwood Mall's Itty Bitty Byte Shop.

"Boy, am I ever glad she did." Inside the computer shop, Carl showed Elaine the modem his stepfather was buying. "How's that for a graduation present?" he asked.

"Nice," said Elaine, trying to feel enthusiasm about the modem. About Carl's stepfather. About *anything*. But even a lazy Sunday afternoon trip to her favorite Glenwood Mall store couldn't seem to pull her out of her funk.

"When I showed him the range of people and companies he could communicate with by computer, he was like a kid in a candy store! All this time I thought he hated computers. It was just that no one had ever taken the time to explain them to him. The only trouble now is I have to share my computer with him." Later, as Carl and Elaine strolled past the mall shops, Carl talked excitedly of his plans for college. He'd been accepted at MIT and the Engineering departments at Michigan and Illinois universities. Elaine half listened. Her mind floated, unfocused.

So, she thought, this is it. This is how it's going to be for me. No great love. No great romance. But, at least, no great pain. She hooked her arm in Carl's, walking with him to Swensen's for ice cream, trying to force her life back to "normal."

Something has changed, thought Elaine. Something is wrong. She was holding Carl's arm, the way she always did. They were walking in the same mall, to the same Swensen's. But Elaine felt a strange undercurrent, like the background music at the opening of *Jaws* which warns there is more in the water than a girl swimming.

Had Elaine really expected things to be the way they were, B.Z.? Before Zack. She heaved a sigh, hugging Carl's arm a bit more tightly. As they waited their turn in the cone line, she studied Carl, who had launched into an animated explanation of his attempt to etch a computer chip to run his bedroom.

"I'm talking turning on lights, pulling drapes..."

This is not going to work, she thought sadly. *Carl is wonderful and caring and special. But I don't feel romantic toward him anymore, and I'm too young to settle for the easy way out.* Maybe there was always pain when you fell in love. Hadn't she suffered pain with Zack, and with Rusty Hughes before him? But risking the hurt had to be better than feeling nothing.

With a shock, Elaine realized her original decision to break up with Carl had nothing to do with Zack Waverly. Even with Zack out of her life, her relationship with Carl was at an end. Suddenly the muddy situation became crystal clear. Zack was out of her life, and the guilt Elaine had felt had gone with him. She was free to look at her relationship with Carl clearly and analytically. And she realized, as much as she liked him, as much as she treasured him as a friend, the romance had been gone from their relationship for a long time.

"Two scoops of vanilla on a Safe-T cone for me," Carl ordered, "and a double rocky road for my mother, here."

The lanky clerk looked up, smiling. Elaine nearly said hello, recognizing Sean Budde, the soft-spoken freshman quarterback. She stopped, realizing he wouldn't recognize her without her Wilbur costume.

"Wait a minute," said Elaine, "make mine tropical coconut swirl."

"Coming right up," said Sean, grabbing a scoop out of the water bucket and heading to the cartons at the far end of the counter.

"You've *never* ordered anything but rocky road," said Carl, puzzled.

"I know," said Elaine, as surprised as Carl at her order. "I just had this craving for tropical coconut swirl."

"Have you ever *tasted* tropical coconut swirl?"

"Nope."

"Daring," he said admiringly. "I can see the headlines in the *Glenwood Call:* Gregory Defies De-tradition."

"What about TV?" she said. "Elaine's Eclectic Eating. Details at ten o'clock."

"First you put orange sherbet in your root beer float and now this. You've inspired me to experiment," he said as Sean returned with their cones.

"Experiment?" Elaine clutched her chest in mock horror. "I don't believe it! You've never, ever eaten anything but vanilla."

"Watch this," he said, turning to Sean, waving his hand with a flourish. "My good man, I want you to reverse my two scoops so the vanilla is on the bottom."

Elaine tried not to laugh at poor Sean's confusion.

"But ... but," he stammered, "*both* scoops are vanilla."

"Ah," Carl said, sighing, taking his cone and studying it appreciatively, "who says you can't find good help anymore? Well done, my man. Well done."

Elaine managed to hold in her laughter until they walked out onto the mall. "He's going to spend the rest of the day trying to figure that one out," she said.

"Good, good," said Carl. "Mind problems stretch the brain. Create character. Put hair on the chest."

"Well, I'll settle for two out of three."

They strolled slowly, leaving the mall and ambling through nearby oak-lined streets. At first, Elaine enjoyed the soft cool breezes, the quiet of the afternoon. Gradually, however, she felt the tension building, tension arising from her decision to break with Carl. The creepy *Jaws* background music played in her mind, and Elaine felt like the shark. She knew what she must do, but she didn't know how. All the scenes she'd created in her mind seemed hokey and contrived. Melodramatic. Silly.

"So," said Carl finally, "how was your tropical coconut swirl?"

"What? Oh ..." Elaine had finished her cone. She didn't remember eating it. "I ... I don't

125

know. All right, I guess."

"'All right, I guess?' For that you gave up rocky road? You *love* rocky road."

"But I know what it tastes like. I wanted to try something new."

"Not better. Just new?"

"I didn't know it wouldn't be better. Oh, Carl. Don't you ever just want to experiment?"

They had come to a small park. They sat next to each other on leather-seated swings, not swinging, just hooking their arms around the chains and swaying slowly back and forth. For a long time, they were silent, watching the patterns their feet made as they dragged in the soft dirt under the swings.

"We aren't talking about ice cream, are we?" Carl asked softly.

Elaine swallowed. There was a rock-hard lump in her throat. This was the most difficult moment of her entire life.

"No," she said. "I guess not."

"I've never been the rocky road of someone's life before." He sighed.

Elaine glanced over hopefully. Could it be that Carl would take this lightly? That he'd help her make this easy? Carl stared unsmiling at his feet. "Funny. You're the vanilla of my life, and I'm totally happy." Elaine looked away.

"You weren't always happy," she reminded him. "Weren't you the one who broke up with me a couple of months ago? The one who thought we should sample other people so, when decision time came, we'd know what we really wanted?"

Carl winced. "I had a feeling that would come back to haunt me," he said. "Have you found some other...other flavor?"

Elaine thought briefly of Zack. "No," she said honestly, "there's no one else. This is between you and me. It's not even something definite I can put my finger on."

"A kind of drawing apart?" Carl asked.

"Yes, exactly that. Have you felt it too?"

"I guess so," said Carl. "I guess I've been trying to pretend it wasn't happening."

Carl turned his swing toward Elaine, and she twisted hers toward him. With eyes lowered, they sat knee to knee.

"This hurts so much," said Elaine, hating the sadness she'd put in his usually twinkling eyes. "If we had fights, or bad experiences, this would make more sense to me."

"Would you feel better if I slugged you?" He tried smiling, but it came out crooked.

"It would sure make breaking up easier," she said, sniffling.

"Breaking up," he said, his voice cracking. "That's what we're doing, isn't it?"

Elaine pressed her lips tightly together, trying to keep control. "I always thought when people broke up there was yelling and screaming and terrible ugly scenes." Her nose was stuffy, and tears welled in her eyes.

"Well, we've never been much like other people."

"The trouble is," she sniffed, "I like you. I like being with you. I can talk to you more easily than just about anyone in the world."

"But you don't have the same feelings you had for me at the beginning."

Elaine was crying softly, steadily. "No," she said, shaking her head from side to side. "I don't. Oh, Carl. I'm so...so...sorry." She wiped her eyes with the back of her hand, but the tears kept coming.

Carl rested his hands palms-up on his knees. Smiling through his tears, he wiggled his fingers invitingly. Slowly, Elaine let go of one chain and then the other, and placed her hands on his.

"In a way," he said gently, "I'm a little relieved."

"Relieved?"

Carl nodded. "I knew our relationship had changed, but I tried to ignore it. I guess I was afraid it was because of something I'd done... or hadn't done. Let's face it, we're both new at this boyfriend-girl friend business. I thought, maybe if I forced myself to be more macho or spontaneous, or—I don't know—all kinds of things."

"I'm glad you didn't change a single thing," said Elaine, reaching out to brush a tear from his cheek, "you're wonderful the way you are."

Carl held her hand, kissing it gently.

"They say you always remember your first girl friend," he said. "I'm glad you were mine."

He stood, helping her up. They hugged tightly, tearfully.

Walking back to the mall, their arms around each other, Elaine felt closer to Carl than she had for weeks.

"Do you think we can still be friends?" she asked as they unlocked their bikes.

"I don't know," said Carl. "I think I'm going to need a little time to heal."

"Just remember," said Elaine, "I'm the only one at school who understands your esoteric sense of humor."

"True," said Carl, swinging a leg over his bike seat.

"And," she said, "I'm the only one on the year-book staff who hasn't thrown something at you when you've come out with one of your pitiful puns."

"I'm in your debt," said Carl. "But, please, let me have time to mourn the death of our relationship."

"Okay," said Elaine, starting off down the hill. "But don't mourn too long. Good friends are mighty hard to come by."

She pedaled down the long, curving road toward her house, racing the wind, racing her thoughts and feelings.

It's over.

It's done.

She thought she'd feel cleansed. Renewed. But all she felt was a strange emptiness inside, as if something very precious had been removed. Something that could never be replaced.

Chapter Eleven

"Andrea locked herself in the bathroom," said Chrissie the moment Elaine walked in the door.

"Yeah, and she won't come out," said Carla. "I had to go and she told me to go in the powder room. I hate the powder room."

"And she's got the phone in there and won't get off."

"And we're expecting a call from Sharon, Karen, and Debbie Herman..."

"So we won't plan our birthday party the same day as theirs..."

"Slow down, slow down," said Elaine, laughing. As usual, the twins made her feel she'd walked into a hurricane. "Take deep breaths." She waited while the twins loudly sucked air in, then let it out in a rush. "That's better. Now,

Chrissie, you start first. Why is Andrea locked in the bathroom?"

Chrissie shrugged her shoulders. "I don't know. Daddy just yelled 'Andrea, stay with the twins!' and she ran up and locked herself in the bathroom."

"She just doesn't want to baby-sit us," said Carla, matter-of-factly. "We're too old to need a sitter, anyway."

Elaine was puzzled. Her parents usually made an effort to be home Sundays. "Where did Dad go?" she asked.

"He had to take Mommy," said Carla. "After she fell down."

Fear jolted Elaine, drenching her body in a cold sweat. She knelt in front of the twins, gripping each by an arm. "What happened?" she asked, trying to keep the fear she was feeling out of her voice.

"Mommy fell on the stairs," said Chrissie. "And Daddy took her to see the doctor."

"She didn't have any scratches," Chrissie called as Elaine bounded up the stairs to Andrea.

"Andrea!" Elaine pounded on the bathroom door. "Andrea, open up!"

Andrea, puffy eyed and sobbing, opened the door slowly. "I'll call you back later," she cried, hanging up the phone. "Oh, Elaine, it was all my f-f-fault," she sobbed.

"Calm down," soothed Elaine. "Now, what

happened?"

"I was s-supposed to take all the odds and ends that had collected on the front stairs up to their proper places. I'd made one trip up and then I got a phone call and then I guess I forgot to bring up the r-rest of the stuff. Mom was coming down the stairs and she stepped on the twins' plastic sticker book. It's so slippery, it just shot out from under her and she crashed down the stairs. Oh, Elaine, it's all my fault."

"It's not your fault," soothed Elaine, putting a comforting arm around her sister.

Elaine's mind raced frantically. She had to get to the hospital. Whom could she call? She dialed Alex, but the Enomotos said Alex was at a diving meet. This is no time to be proud, Elaine told herself. Taking a deep breath, she dialed Karen. Elaine, embarrassed at making a fool of herself at the festival, had been avoiding Karen all week.

"McGillicutty's Peruvian Laundry and Toenail Clipping Service," said a British voice.

"Karen? It's Elaine." Quickly, she explained what had happened.

"I'll be right there," said Karen. It wasn't until Elaine hung up that she realized Zack might have answered the phone. *That's all I would have needed,* she thought.

"Come on," she said to Andrea, taking her to the sink. Elaine wiped a cool washcloth over Andrea's face, then down along the back of her neck. "You've got to calm down. Crying won't help Mom, and we mustn't frighten the twins."

"I-I'll try," said Andrea.

"That's better," said Elaine.

As she followed Andrea down the stairs, Elaine thought of the scene from *Gone With the Wind* in which a pregnant Scarlett O'Hara falls down a flight of stairs and has a miscarriage. She shivered. She tried to block out the scene, but she'd seen the movie at least a dozen times, and the image of Scarlett falling played over and over in her mind.

For the first time, Elaine truly understood the depth of the guilt Karen felt when Mrs. Waverly had miscarried. Like Karen, Elaine hadn't wanted her mother to have a baby. She understood now how tragic it would be if her mother really did lose the baby. A loud horn blew out in front.

"That's Karen," said Elaine. "Take care of the twins. I'll call as soon as I find out anything."

Mr. Gregory stood in the corridor outside the emergency room. His baggy Sunday "knock-around" pants and shirt that looked so comfortable at home made him look shabby and vulnerable in the sterile hospital hall. Elaine rushed into his arms, and he hugged her tightly.

"It's all right, it's all right," he soothed. "Mom's a little shaken up and bruised, but she's going to be just fine. Just fine."

"And . . . and the baby," she asked fearfully.

"Your brother?" Her father's face lifted in a huge smile. "The doctor says he's one hundred percent. Looks like he's one tough kid."

"My brother?" Elaine said, laughing and crying. "But how . . ."

"Those tests the doctor ran last week for birth defects? The results were here in the lab. A side benefit is you get to find out if the baby's going to have indoor or outdoor plumbing."

"Daddy," Elaine said, embarrassed.

"Looks like I'm finally going to have another man around the house."

Elaine couldn't believe how much younger and healthier her father looked. For the first time, he had the glow he'd had before the terrible time when he was out of work. In fact, both her parents looked ten years younger since her mother had become pregnant. *How could I have been so selfish*, wondered Elaine. This baby is exactly what her parents needed. It marked a new beginning for them. Elaine said a silent prayer of thanks that her brother survived the fall. She glowed in the warm rush of love she felt for the new baby.

"I don't think I've ever seen you this happy," Elaine said, tenderly brushing back a strand of his thinning blond hair.

"You should have seen the laugh lines in this old face the day *you* were born," he said. A nurse beckoned him from down the hall, and he motioned for the girls to wait.

"I'm going to have a brother!" Elaine said, grabbing Karen and swinging her around. "A brother!"

"If I knew you wanted one so badly," laughed Karen, "I'd have given you one of mine."

"Mom's doing fine," said Mr. Gregory. "They're going to keep her here for a while, and I'm going to wait. But I want you to call Andrea and the twins with the good news. Then the two of you go on home."

It wasn't until they were well on the way home that Elaine felt overcome by the emotional upheavals of the day. Her body felt like lead, and she leaned back in the seat, closing her eyes.

"I broke up with Carl, today...."

"Oh, you poor kid," said Karen. "This has not been one of your best days. Why did you break up?" Karen asked cautiously. "Was it because of Zack?"

"No. Not that I didn't wonder about that, myself. But I had outgrown my relationship with Carl. It was over. With or without Zack."

"And now," said Karen, "what do you feel for Zack?"

Elaine opened her eyes, staring as the streets of Glenwood rushed by them.

"I guess I still feel the way I did before I saw Zack with his girl friend. Zack is very special, and I miss him. But there's a layer of hurt on top of the love I felt. And it's painful for me to think about him, now."

"Is that why you haven't been answering his phone calls?"

Elaine nodded. "I think it's better if I just let things wind down of their own accord."

Karen listened, strangely subdued, occasionally offering sympathetic comments.

A few times, Elaine questioned Karen about Zack's girl friend, but Karen hadn't offered a single piece of information. It seemed strange to Elaine since Karen was usually eager to discuss anyone at any time.

She doesn't want to hurt me with the truth, Elaine decided—the truth that Zack was and always had been in love with the beautiful, thin, long-haired blonde.

Sunday night.
Eating cold mac and cheese from the pot in the fridge.
(My friends think I don't eat. They should see me at night!)

Dear Journal,
(I really must give you another name. "Journal" is so impersonal.)

Big scare today! Mom slipped on the stairs. Luckily, she and my brother are fine. A brother! I can't even imagine what that will be like. Do you realize that if I had a baby now, it will have an uncle the same age?

Not that there's any chance of that happening. Not only am I—ahem—"inexperienced" (pay attention, great-granddaughters!), but I don't even have a boyfriend. Not anymore. Not since today. Carl and I are now history. A lovely, wonderful history, but history nonetheless.

I owe you an apology. A week ago I said you were a dumb idea. Right now I can't imagine how I would have survived this crazy week without you. Especially since most of my crises came at weird hours. I doubt my friends would have liked me calling at four in the morning to tell them I had cramps.

That's not true. They'd come if I needed them, no matter what time it was. Of course, Kit's such a sound sleeper she wouldn't even hear the phone ring. And Lori's so sympathetic she'd probably bake something and rush it right over. Alex would ask those blunt questions of hers. And I don't always know the answers.

I actually did give Karen a crisis call today for a ride to the hospital (You remember, Zack's sister), but I mustn't do that again. You-know-who might answer. It will be awhile (like a lifetime) before I can listen to the sound of his voice . . .

. . . and not think of a dead goldfish . . .

. . . and not start crying all over again.
Your friend, Elaine
(the Heartbreaker — the Heartbroken)

Chapter Twelve

"If I see one more couple holding hands," growled Elaine, "I'm going to scream."

She and Alex squeezed through the lunchtime crowd to their lockers.

"I know how you feel," said Alex. "There's something tragic about an unheld hand."

Elaine sidestepped a football-tossing group of boys. "Ohhhhh!" she cried, bashing full force into an open locker door.

"Hey, watch it," said the couple that had been embracing in the shadows of the locker.

"Sorry," she said, feeling her bruised upper lip swelling. "Alex, is *everyone* at Glenwood in love?"

"It just seems that way when you break up." Alex spun open her combination lock, digging through her collection of swimsuits in search of her lunch bag. "That's how I felt when I broke up with Danny ... and with Wes." Elaine noticed the tremor in Alex's voice as she mentioned the handsome race car driver.

"It's my own fault for breaking up with Carl," said Elaine.

"I tried to warn you."

Elaine opened her locker, stared inside for a while, and closed it. "I know I did the right thing, Alex. But that sure doesn't make it any easier." She started toward the quad.

"Ummm, Elaine?" Alex leaned against the lockers, her dark eyes twinkling mischievously.

"Yes?"

"Don't you think it would be easier to eat your lunch if you took it out of your locker?"

"Oh." Elaine quickly retrieved her lunch. "I'm becoming a real space cadet."

"It's just spring fever," said Alex. She steered Elaine toward the shady, grassy spot Kit and her boyfriend, Justin Kennerly, had saved for them.

"That's what Carl said I had," said Elaine. "If this is spring fever, I have a feeling I'm in for one heck of a long spring."

Thinking of Carl gave Elaine a sad feeling inside. The few times she'd seen him that week, he'd looked tired and draggy, like a deflated balloon. Although on Thursday she'd seen him walking Patti Hamu to class, and he'd been carrying on an unusually animated conversation. Maybe shy, quiet Patti was just the type to bring out the aggressive side of Carl.

"The Romans really knew how to eat grapes," said Justin. His mop of sandy blond curls rested in Kit's lap as he contentedly nibbled the grapes she dangled over his mouth.

"You're spoiling him," warned Lori, who sat like a prim Southern belle in the swirl of her full gauzy skirt. She daintily separated her daily orange into sections. Now that she had landed a few jobs as a hand model, she was super cautious about damaging her fingernails. "If you aren't careful, pretty soon he'll want you to peel the grapes for him."

"Now why didn't *I* think of that?" asked Justin.

"Because you're charming, intelligent, and sensitive," said Kit, dropping a grape on his nose. "And you wouldn't press your luck."

"Ah, yes." Justin sighed. "Now I remember."

"Another happy couple," moaned Elaine. "Do I need this?"

"You were right," conceded Alex. "The whole world is two by two."

Elaine's eyes swept the couple-filled quad. "Where's Noah when you really need him?"

"Hang in there," said Lori. "All breakups are painful in their own way, but the first time's the hardest. If it's any consolation, we've all been through breakups at least once."

143

"Once a day's more like it," said Karen, flopping down near Elaine. "For some of us, anyway." She emptied her lunch from her oversized shoulder bag. "It's when Jeff and I *aren't* breaking up that I really begin to worry."

"The readjustment process takes time," Alex assured Elaine. "I was so miserable for weeks after I broke up with Danny. And I'm still dreaming about Wes...and that's when I'm *awake.*"

Kit laughed and nodded her agreement. "It's never easy," she said, running her fingers lovingly through Justin's hair.

"Actually," said Elaine, "I don't think I'm hurting because of the breakup. I just feel funny. Floaty. Like one hand clapping."

"I thought everyone felt like that," said Karen, wide-eyed in comic surprise. She took out a black felt-tip pen and drew a zipper on a banana. "What you need is to see a great new movie," she said. "Here, unzip this for me, will you."

"I hardly think..." Elaine started to protest.

"Something you've never seen before, to get your mind off...things."

"Karen, I've seen every movie out," said Elaine. The others laughed as she carefully "unzipped" the banana.

"I've got a film you've never seen," said Karen mysteriously, glancing around as if to be sure she wasn't overheard. "It's so underground it's beyond cult."

"I don't know..." Elaine hedged. "I don't feel much like going out. Where's it playing?"

"My house," said Karen. "I've got it on my VCR. Come on over tonight after work."

"I'm not sure," Elaine said, not wanting to hurt Karen's feelings, but not wanting to run into Zack, either. "Let me think about it."

After lunch, Elaine and Karen walked across the quad to class. In the distance Karen saw Carl walking and laughing with Patti Hamu.

"Looks like Carl's regrouped," said Karen. "That was some short mourning period."

"He could have been unhappy just a *little* longer," said Elaine, feeling as if the last thin thread connecting her to Carl had snapped. "I think I'll take a pass on that movie, Karen. I'm afraid I'm not very good company just now."

"That's the beauty of friends," said Karen, "you don't have to be 'on' all the time. That's why I like being with you and why I'm lucky to have Jeff. I know I make a big deal out of guys like Silvano and the Ping-Pong player, but the truth is, I'm not at all relaxed with them."

"Then why do you flirt with them?"

Karen shrugged her shoulders. "I guess I need to know that boys find me attractive—that a funny-faced character like me can compete with the heavy hitters."

Elaine knew it was useless to try to convince Karen she was attractive. Elaine remembered when her friends told her she was pretty. She hadn't believed them. She thought of herself as "a brain," as if her brain weren't attached to a body. Karen thought of herself as a "funny girl": Barbra Streisand playing Fanny Brice.

"I don't understand you," said Elaine. "You were so happy when Jeff started taking you seriously. Why risk jeopardizing your relationship by flirting with other guys?"

"Landing Jeff was the important thing. It's weird. I fight to get a guy's attention, and then, once he likes me, I wonder how good his taste can be. As Groucho once said"—she fingered an imaginary cigar—"'I wouldn't belong to any club that would have me as a member.' Which reminds me, are you coming to see the movie, or what?"

"I don't quite see the connection," said Elaine, laughing. "But all right. The idea of spending the entire weekend alone isn't very appealing. Maybe a movie would be a good idea. Will, uh, anyone else be at your house with us?"

"No. I doubt this movie would interest anyone else I know. It's really weird."

"Thanks a lot."

"And Zack and Mom are taking Fred used-car shopping."

Relief swept over Elaine. She had been avoiding Karen's house because she feared running into Zack.

"Are there any car chases in this movie?"

Elaine asked cautiously. "I think that's my biggest pet peeve, right after couples jumping into bed the minute they're introduced."

"Not one single car flying over one single bed." Karen laughed. "Promise."

The Waverly house smelled of freshly popped popcorn, which rested in a huge bowl on the sofa between Karen and Elaine. Two dogs from the Waverlys' menagerie curled up contentedly at the girls' feet as they settled in for the film. Karen loaded the tape player, pressed the remote control, and the screen suddenly brightened with a close-up of Zack.

Elaine choked on her popcorn, coughing and sputtering as a laughing Karen pounded her on her back.

"Hello, Elaine," said Zack, smiling.

"Karen," coughed Elaine, unable to sound as angry as she felt. Karen shrugged innocently, turning back to the screen.

"Since you wouldn't see me or talk to me," said Zack, "I had to think of some way to get your attention. Not that I haven't enjoyed my long involved phone conversations with Andrea, but I really don't call your home to talk to your little sister. Little sisters can be so..." His eyes shifted to where Karen sat. "Sorry, Karen. Forgot you were there."

"I'll bet," said Karen, throwing a handful of popcorn at the screen. As soon as the kernels fell to the floor, they were promptly devoured by the delighted dogs.

"Anyway," said Zack, "I had to find a way to make you listen. I sure hope you are, that you're not turning me off with the remote control. I think we've been too far apart for too long as it is. I think it's time we got together."

Elaine stared, openmouthed, as Zack explained. "That girl you saw me with at the film festival used to be my girl friend. I was on the verge of breaking up with her when I met you."

He paused, his eyes looking directly at Elaine. She could see the truth in them, and it sent shivers racing through her.

"I was wrong not to have broken up with her completely before I began calling you each night. Maybe that was a throwback to all those years I had no one. What I did was weak and immature, and I apologize."

"You never apologize to me!" complained Karen, tossing more popcorn at him.

"Shhhh!" said Elaine, afraid to miss a single word.

"I broke up with that girl the night of the festival. I've outgrown the need to hold on to someone I don't want until someone better comes along. Remember I told you I'd reached a point where I'd begun to think about the type of girl I really wanted?"

"Yes," Elaine whispered.

"Well, I've been giving that a great deal of

thought. If you haven't totally given up on me by now," he continued, "I'm hoping I can ask you to do me a big favor...."

"What?" cried Elaine, forgetting she was talking to a TV screen.

Zack's face faded as the tape ended and the screen filled with static.

Elaine turned questioningly to the grinning Karen. "Don't look at me," said Karen innocently, "although I do seem to remember Zack saying that if you want to hear the rest, you should meet him at the ... the, uh ... let me see, the ..."

"Karen!" Elaine shrieked. "Stop kidding around. Please. Where *is* he?"

"I don't see why you're attracted to ..."

"I'm going to pulverize you," Elaine threatened, laughing.

"No accounting for taste." Karen shrugged. "Anyway, he's down the block at the Sher-Main Grill."

Elaine jumped up, rushing to the door. Catching her reflection in the entry hall mirror, she stopped to quickly repair her hair and makeup from the day's ravages of school and work. Oh why hadn't she washed her hair that morning? And couldn't she have worn something more exciting than white jeans and a blouse? Karen came and stood behind her, grinning broadly.

"Why didn't you *tell* me?" asked Elaine, quickly brushing on a light coating of blush. "You must have known what he was up to. How could you have let me be so miserable all week?"

"Zack made me promise not to say anything."

"But, I'm your friend!"

"Sure, but Zack's my brother, and he said if I told you about this he'd chaperone every one of my dates for the next ten years. What kind of guy is going to kiss me with my gorilla of a brother sitting in the back seat of the car?"

"You're a devil," said Elaine. "And an angel." Giving Karen a quick hug, she raced her bike down the long winding hill to the Sher-Main Grill.

The cigar-chomping owner was mopping up, getting ready to close. Elaine saw Zack in the back booth. When he saw her, his face burst into a mixture of relief and desire that made Elaine's legs feel wobbly. She forced herself to walk toward him calmly, even though her thudding heart felt as if it were about to explode.

"Excuse me," she said, standing at the booth, "but don't I know you from somewhere?"

Zack eased himself out of the booth and stood in front of her. Silently, he slipped his arms around her and pulled her to him.

"You might have seen me in a movie," he said, his loving eyes caressing her face.

"Yes." She nodded, swallowing nervously. "I think that may be it."

Zack kissed her lips softly.

"Is that your heart beating or mine?" she

asked, putting her arms around his neck.

"Sounds like a duet," he said huskily, kissing her more deeply.

"A-hem." The man with the mop coughed loudly, shifting the cigar from one side of his mouth to the other. "Sorry, Zack, but I been here since four in the ay-em. Gotta get back to the missus."

Zack looked up without releasing Elaine. "Okay, Gus. Thanks for staying open for me. I owe you one."

"Looks like she was worth the wait." Gus winked. Elaine looked down, embarrassed.

"You're a real blusher, aren't you," said Zack. Elaine felt her face go from warm to hot. "There are so many things I want to learn about you." He smiled. "Come on."

He took her hand and led her outside. They strolled across the street to a small park. Zack took her in his arms again.

"On the video you said you wanted me to do you a big favor," Elaine said, slipping her arms around his waist, unable to believe she was really able to hold him at last. "What is it?"

"I'm hoping"—Zack took her face in his hands, his deep blue eyes searching hers—"that you can tell me how my movie ends. Does the guy get the girl?"

"Does the guy want the girl?" asked Elaine, her nervous voice barely a whisper.

"More than he's ever wanted anyone in his

life."

"Well, then"—Elaine sighed deeply—"who are we to deny them a happy ending?"

This time their kiss was long and intense, and Elaine lost all sense of time and space.

"And they lived happily ever after," Zack whispered in her ear. "Or has that been done?"

"Never by us," Elaine said, happily resting her head on his chest. "Never by us."

Friday night.
Or is it Saturday morning?
Who knows? Who cares?
I see a zillion and one stars through my bed-
room skylight—and they're all winking at me.

    I'M IN LOVE!
    ZACK'S IN LOVE!
    We're in love with each other.
    At the same time.

Oh, "J" (like your new name?),
    I know this must seem very confusing to you
since I've only told you bits and pieces of
what's been going on in my life.
    I promise to do better. Truly. I will write

reams and reams about Zack and me and everything we do. (Well, maybe not quite everything. After all, a great-grandmother should have some secrets.)

Zack just left and I can't wait to see him again. I'd better bring the phone up here. He's going to call me as soon as he gets home.

Look how shaky my writing is. I'm trembling. Does everyone in love feel this way? I can't believe anyone has ever felt this way. I'm the first! I have to be! I have single-handedly discovered LOVE and it is FABULOUS.

Must bring up the phone.

I love you. I love the world. I love life. And most of all

I LOVE ZACK WAVERLY

Your friend for life,

Elaine (Zack's Girl)